T0209033

DEATH BY MUSHROOM

TOM KROPP

BALBOA.PRESS
A DIVISION OF HAY HOUSE

Balboa Press books may be ordered through booksellers or by contacting:

Balboa Press
A Division of Hay House
1663 Liberty Drive
Bloomington, IN 47403
www.balboapress.com
844-682-1282

Because of the dynamic nature of the Internet, any web addresses or links contained in this book may have changed since publication and may no longer be valid. The views expressed in this work are solely those of the author and do not necessarily reflect the views of the publisher, and the publisher hereby disclaims any responsibility for them.

The author of this book does not dispense medical advice or prescribe the use of any technique as a form of treatment for physical, emotional, or medical problems without the advice of a physician, either directly or indirectly. The intent of the author is only to offer information of a general nature to help you in your quest for emotional and spiritual well-being. In the event you use any of the information in this book for yourself, which is your constitutional right, the author and the publisher assume no responsibility for your actions.

Any people depicted in stock imagery provided by Getty Images are models, and such images are being used for illustrative purposes only. Certain stock imagery © Getty Images.

Print information available on the last page.

ISBN: 978-1-9822-6296-9 (sc)
ISBN: 978-1-9822-6298-3 (hc)
ISBN: 978-1-9822-6297-6 (e)

Library of Congress Control Number: 2021902714

Balboa Press rev. date: 02/09/2021

I thank Darlene O'Connell without whose help this book would have been a mess. Her editing ability and encouragement gave me the nerve to continue.

DISCLAIMER

The characters in this tome are figments of the author's imagination. They in no way represent any person living or not. Similarities are merely coincidental.

CONTENTS

Chapter 1...1

Chapter 2...5

Chapter 3...7

Chapter 4...11

Chapter 5...13

Chapter 6...14

Chapter 7...18

Chapter 8...20

Chapter 9...23

Chapter 10...26

Chapter 11...29

Chapter 12...33

Chapter 13...36

Chapter 14...37

Chapter 15...40

Chapter 16...42

Chapter 17...43

Chapter 18...46

Chapter 19...47

Chapter 20...48

Chapter 21...53

Chapter 22...56

Chapter 23...58

Chapter 24...60

Chapter 25 63
Chapter 26 65
Chapter 27 70
Chapter 28 73
Chapter 29 75
Chapter 30 78
Chapter 31 80
Chapter 32 83
Chapter 33 85
Chapter 34 86
Chapter 35 88
Chapter 36 94
Chapter 37 96
Chapter 38 97
Chapter 39 102
Chapter 40 106
Chapter 41 109
Chapter 42 111
Chapter 43 113
Chapter 44 117
Chapter 45 119
Chapter 46 122
Chapter 47 124
Chapter 48 126
Chapter 49 129
Chapter 50 131
Chapter 51 133
Chapter 52 136

CHAPTER 1

Robert J. Vanderburgh Sr., CEO of Vanderburgh Electronics, age fifty-seven, was contemplating a hostile takeover of his archenemy and primary rival in Michigan, Tamarac Electronics.

Vanderburgh was poring over the latest stock quotes and the amount of outstanding Tamarac shares available on the market. He was about ten thousand shares short of holding a majority ownership of Tamarac. None of those who held those shares had any intentions of selling, nor could they be persuaded to vote his way on the hostile takeover.

He fretted about what to do next. That's when he felt a nagging pain in his chest. At first, it was just a dull ache, but it lingered. He thought it might just be indigestion, so he took one of the many antacids he took daily. The pain was not relieved, so he chewed another one thinking it would work faster, but that one too offered no relief. The pain was getting worse. His left arm started to tingle; the left side of jaw went slack and began to hurt.

He still thought it was nothing. Then it hit. Excruciating pain in the left side of his chest, down his arm, and up to his neck and jaw. He looked up at no one with a puzzled look and fell face-down on his desk nearly slipping out of his chair. He was dead.

In the morning, Clara Barton, his secretary of many years, was concerned because he hadn't come blustering in at precisely 9:00 a.m. throwing the usual orders around. She got up to investigate.

She opened the door a crack expecting to see Mr. V at his desk poring over papers. Not seeing him right away, she opened the door farther. When she saw him, she nearly passed out.

Gathering her composure, she called the chief of security chief, Tom Davis, a retired Marine Master Gunnery Sergeant. Tom was burly and ruggedly handsome; he was wanted by all the single women in the building and probably some of the married ones too. "Tom, you need to come here immediately."

When Tom sauntered into the office, he saw Clara sobbing hysterically. He looked into Mr. Vanderburgh's office and found him in the same position as he had been when Clara first saw him. He calmly walked over to Mr. Vanderburgh's desk, felt for a pulse, and said to no one in particular, "Yep, he's dead." He picked up the phone with a handkerchief and used a pencil to dial 911.

"911 operator. What's your emergency?"

"There isn't exactly an emergency. Please send the coroner and the homicide detectives to Vanderburgh Electronics, Mr. Vanderburgh's office. There isn't any hurry. He's dead."

"Okay, I'll get someone right there."

A few minutes later, sirens announced the arrival of an ambulance, the coroner, and police; they were ushered in through the main gate of Vanderburgh Electronics.

Detective Sergeant Ronald Flores glared first at the body and then at Tom. "Why did you call me in on this one? It's a case of a bad ticker. You didn't move or touch anything, did you?"

"You sure about that, Sarge? Mr. V was a fit man. Ran three miles every day, ate right, wasn't overweight. Just got a clean bill of health from his doctor," Tom said.

"Yeah, I'm sure. With as many stiffs as I've seen in my career, you'd think I'd know a murder from natural causes by now."

"Okay, Sarge. Just keep that in mind when I investigate and find the murderer," said Tom.

"Oh I will. Two weeks from now, you'll come to me with hat in hand to apologize."

The coroner determined that Robert Sr. had died approximately twelve hours before being discovered. The coroner's preliminary ruling was death by infarction; that was a quick assessment based on the position of the body, no evidence of a break-in, and no visible trauma.

Clara called Mrs. Vivian Vanderburgh, Robert Jr., and Madeline Grath, Robert Jr's married sister who arrived just as the coroner was preparing the body for transport to the morgue. Mrs. V and Madeline were in bad shape. Tears streaming down their lovely faces were streaking their mascara, eye shadow, and blush. Puffy red eyes indicated they had been crying almost nonstop since they had heard the news.

Camera and news crews were beginning to assemble outside the fences of Vanderburgh Electronics trying in vain to catch a glimpse of the devastated family. The nosy, perverted piranhas trying to get the story of the great man's demise were being foiled by the fence and shrubs surrounding the property.

The caravan of Detective Sergeant Flores, the coroner's van, and a squad car with lights flashing and sirens blaring left the compound. The Vanderburgh's car was sandwiched in the middle. They headed to the morgue where the coroner, Dr. Melvin Blumenstein, would perform the autopsy. Paparazzi followed but couldn't get close enough because the caravan was traveling with a police escort.

The Vanderburgh's limo peeled off to return home to plan for the funeral as the procession approached the morgue.

"I don't care what you say. Father is not going to be cremated. He is going to be buried in the family plot at United Memorial Gardens," insisted Robert.

"No, he wanted to be cremated to save the environment. He wanted his ashes to be scattered over the Detroit River," Madeline said.

"How would you know? Since you got married to that fortune

hunter, you've hardly been around. You never show up at family functions," said Robert.

"Stop it both of you!" Vivian shouted. "Your father has just passed away. We don't know where your brother is, and you're bickering like always!" Calming down somewhat, she continued. "We'll wait until the reading of the will. I'll call his lawyer in a few minutes to arrange it. Until then, there will be no more discussion on how your father will be put to rest. Robert, call the pastor and make arrangements for the funeral service. There will be a service regardless of what your father's wishes were or how he wanted to be put to rest. Madeline, I want you to arrange the funeral dinner."

"Mother, what if father didn't want a service? You know how private he tried to be in church," Robert said.

"I said there would be a service, and that's that. You have your assignments. Get to them. Oh, and Robert, see if you can find your brother. Get him sobered up so he can at least attend the service."

"Momma, what do you want for the funeral dinner? How many should I plan for? Will drinking be allowed? Should it be a large dinner, or just finger food, or maybe a light lunch?" Madeline asked in a whiny tone.

"Dear, I told *you* to do the planning. If I told you all that, I'd be doing the planning, wouldn't I?"

"But Momma, I don't know anything about this planning stuff. I wouldn't know where to begin."

"Well young lady, it's about time you learned."

Each went about his or her business albeit ruefully and reluctantly.

CHAPTER 2

Vivian called her late husband's lawyer, Harold Pfeiffer.

"Harold, this is Vivian. Robert just died. We need a will reading right away. The sooner the better."

"Ahh, Umm. Yeah. Okay, I guess."

"What do you mean you guess? There is a will, isn't there?"

"Yes, but Rob amended it."

"Amended?"

"Yes, Vivian, amended."

"How could he amend it? We had agreed to his will. He can't change it after all the work I put into it. How has he *amended* it?"

"Vivian, I can't tell you until the official reading. I can arrange it for a few days from now."

"I need it done now! This afternoon! Cancel whatever else you had planned. I want you to come over here and read the darned thing now!"

"Vivian, I can't do that. I have to wait to see if the death was natural or if foul play was involved. That's part of the will-reading instructions. Another one is that all family members must be present. Is Rory available? I can't read it until you find him and get him here sober or not."

"That's just absurd! I don't know if Rory's drunk or sober, high or not, or dead or alive never mind where he is. That could take days. I need the will read now."

"What's the rush, Vivian? The will certainly isn't going anywhere, and it can't be changed now."

"Yes, I suppose you're right."

CHAPTER 3

Robert went back to work to make sure that the plant was humming as usual, that no one was slacking off because the old man had died. He wanted them to know that he was in charge and that business would go on as usual.

The first phone call was to maintenance.

"I want the name on my father's office changed immediately to mine and the title to CEO and CFO. I want the old man's personal things taken out of there. The furniture can stay. Then move my things into that office."

"Yes sir Mr. Vanderburgh, right away."

The next order of business was to terminate Clara.

"Clara, could you come to my office, please?"

"Sure, Mr. V. Do you want me to bring a pen and paper?"

"That won't be necessary."

Clara walked to Robert's office only to realize that it was empty. A maintenance man was there, so Clara asked him what was going on. He informed her that Robert had moved into his father's office. Clara scurried back to the main building, where Robert Sr.'s office was. She went to his office and knocked. Robert invited her in.

"Sit down, Clara. Can I get you something? Coffee? Water? A drink?"

"No sir. Thank you. I'm fine."

She wondered what was up; he was treating her way too kindly. Maybe it was because he was grieving, she thought.

"Clara, I know you've been with the company for a long time now ... What is it? ... Thirty years?"

"Thirty-two, sir. I've been with your father since he opened the place when he was just twenty-five."

"So, what does that make you now? Sixty? Sixty-five?"

"Thank you for the compliment, but I'll be seventy in a month."

"Well, you certainly look good for someone your *age*."

"Yes, I try to stay in shape."

"Have you ever thought of retiring?"

"Not on your life. I like working with your father. I mean liked working for him."

"Other than that, why haven't you retired?"

"I can't afford it," she answered bluntly.

"Working for my father, you must have made a decent salary. Well above industry in general."

"Yes sir, yes I did."

"Didn't you save anything?"

"I wasn't able to, sir. But I don't think I like the tone of the conversation or where it's headed."

"I'm rather curious why a single woman can't save at least part of her salary."

"Sir, that's none of your business."

"It's gambling, isn't it?"

"Certainly not. I haven't gambled a day in my life. I resent your implication."

"I'm sorry, Clara. Why don't you tell me what happened to all your money? Maybe I can help."

"I doubt that. Harry, my husband, and I had a child who was born with a multitude of problems. She needed all sorts of hospitalizations, operations, specialized medicine. Your father paid for it all until Harry died fifteen years ago. Why he stopped, I don't know. Anyway, I have had to foot most of the bills since then. I've run out of what savings Harry and I had to keep Samantha in a good home not far from where I live. I can't care for her myself anymore."

"What would it take to get you to retire, Clara? How much do you have to pay for the nursing home?"

"I give the nursing home all of Sam's disability income, and that covers about a third. My church has been able to provide some, but I have to pay about thirty-five hundred a month."

"How much do you get paid a month?"

"After taxes and insurance, five thousand two hundred and fifty."

"Would you consider retiring if I were to pay you a hundred thousand annually until you pass away?"

"That's only about two thousand more than I make a month. I'd still have to make up the remaining fifteen hundred. How would I do that? Who would take care of my daughter after I pass?"

"How about I set up a trust fund payable when you pass away to the conservator of your choice?"

"What amount are you proposing?"

"What do you think is a reasonable figure?"

"Well, I don't know. That depends on how generous you're feeling."

"Let's not go overboard."

"I won't, Sonny. Ya see, I'm your boss."

"How can you be? I own this place."

"No, you don't. Your father knew you'd try to take over after he was gone, but he didn't want you to run the company into the ground. Just before he died, he had his will changed and bequeathed me fifty-one percent of the outstanding stock. So you see, sonny, if you're trying to get rid of me, you can't. I on the other hand can get rid of you."

"He can't do that! I'll contest the will! He has no right. You have no right. I'm his son!"

"Yes, you are, sonny. And you better get used to the idea that I'll be your boss as soon as the will is read. By the way, get your stuff out of my office and back to yours, and change that hideous door."

Robert stomped out of the office like the spoiled brat he was. He went to the maintenance shed grumbling all the way to get them to change the offices back to the way they were.

Meanwhile, Madeline wasn't having any success. She went to the caterer who had done her coming-out party to see what they could do for her. Since her last party had become such a mess with the caterer losing several hundred dollars, they wouldn't even talk to her. It seems that the catering business was a closed clique; no one else would give her the time of day.

She thought about having an old-fashioned potluck but thought better of it when she realized how her mother would react to that idea. She went home and threw one of her infamous temper tantrums. She threw out all of the china and crystal. When her unsuspecting hubby got home, she lit into him like a Roman candle on the Fourth of July. Harry made the mistake of asking her what was wrong.

"What's wrong? What's wrong? I'll tell you what's wrong. Daddy had the nerve to die today, and Mother wants me to make the arrangements for the funeral dinner. I don't have the slightest idea how to do that, and Mommy dearest won't tell me anything. She expects me to do it myself.

"None of the caterers will talk to me. I even thought of a potluck. At least I could get the ladies at the church to organize the thing and run it. I may ask one of them anyway. No, Mother would kill me and then expect me to arrange for my funeral dinner. My daddy left me all alone!" she said with a sob as she collapsed into his arms and bawled.

CHAPTER 4

Tamara Hayes was an up-and-coming young electrical engineer with a degree from the Lawrence University of Technology just outside Detroit. She was well known in the electronics industry, but she was an enigma to most who know her.

Beautiful and light skinned, she didn't seem to be attracted to any man or woman for that matter. She rarely if ever dated anyone. If she did, it was to further her career and business. The real intrigue and draw were her eyes—mint-green with flecks of gold, catlike, piercing, yet gentle when she wanted them to be.

Hayes was sitting at her desk reading the *Detroit News* when the headline jumped out at her: "Electronics Mogul Dies." She quickly read the story.

> Electronics mogul Robert J. Vanderburgh Sr. died at his desk last night of an apparent heart attack. Police have no details at this time and are still investigating. According to a police spokesman, there were no signs of a break-in, a struggle, or trauma on the body. At this point, the cause of death would only be conjecture. Mr. V, as many called Vanderburgh, grew up locally and graduating from Wayne Memorial High School and Sienna Heights University. Shortly after high school ….

She stopped reading there. She wondered how much it would cost to buy out Vanderburgh Electronics. She called her accountant, Winton Flowers.

"Winton, I'd like to see you right away concerning a business proposal I'm thinking about."

"Let me check my schedule to see what I have available," Winton said.

"If you can make it this afternoon or early tonight …"

"I think I can make it around three this afternoon."

"Pencil that in. I have to get hold of Harold and see if he can be here too. I'll get back to you."

Tamara figured out what to tell Harold since he was also the Vanderburgh's lawyer, and she gave him a call. "Harold, Tamara here."

"Yes Tamara. How are you, dear? We don't get together enough. You didn't call, though, just to chitchat. What's on your mind?"

"I'd like to see you around three this afternoon if that's convenient. I want to discuss a business opportunity that's come up. Winton will be there too. Maybe we can have an early dinner at Benihana's."

"Let me look … Yeah, that looks good. Should I meet you there or at your office?"

"There would be fine."

They hung up, and Tamara called Winton back to let him know about the arrangements.

CHAPTER 5

Rory Vanderburgh, the wayward child, was at his favorite bar, the Do Drop Inn, slugging down his tenth Budweiser. The bartender was just about to cut him off when Robert strolled through the door looking for him. Momentarily blinded by stepping into the dark bar from the bright sunlight, Robert didn't immediately see his brother.

The bartender sidled over to Rory. "Hey Rory, if you don't what to be found, slip behind me and go out the back door. Your brother just came in. I don't think he's seen you yet."

"Thanks, man. I owe you one," slurred Rory as he left.

Robert waltzed up to the bar confidently like a man who was used to getting what he wanted. "Hey barkeep, have you seen my drunkard of a brother?"

"No, Mr. Vanderburgh, not today. You might check that fleabag motel down the road. I heard he was shacking up with some cocaine addict and they were having a good ol' time of it. Can I get you a drink?"

"No. I'm just looking for Rory. If you see him, tell him I need him to call me at this number right away." He scribbled his number on a bar napkin. "Tell him it's an emergency. Dial it for him if he's too drunk to do it himself. Prop him up if you have to."

CHAPTER 6

Tamara's lawyer and accountant met just outside Benihana's and were pleased to see one another.

"Hello, Winton. How are you?" asked Harold.

"I'm fine. I thought you were the Vanderburgh's lawyer. Why are you here?"

"I am their lawyer. I also represent Tammy. I might ask you the same thing. What brings you to our neck of the woods? Slumming?"

"Tammy told me she wanted to talk about some business deal. She rarely consults me unless it's already done and she wants opinions and how to pay for it."

"I hear you. Tammy usually talks to me before negotiations go very far. I wonder what she's up to now. Did you hear about the old man Vanderburgh?"

"No."

"He died sometime last night."

"No kidding! Wow! He wasn't that old. I figured he'd be around a lot longer wheeling and dealing."

"Yeah, so did I."

They lapsed into silence as they thought about the events of the day and what had yet to occur.

Tamara was standing at the door as they went in. "Hello, gentlemen. Would you care to follow me? I got a private room so we could talk in peace."

The waiter followed them into the room and asked, "Would anyone like anything from the bar? May I suggest mai tais? They're excellent, and today, you can get them for half off before five o'clock."

"No thank you. We have some business to discuss," stated Tammy.

"In that case, may I suggest iced green tea. Soothing and calming to the nerves and mellows one's insights."

"Would you for now bring us some iced water? Thank you." Tammy dismissed him. "Okay boys, let's get down to business. We can order later. Here's what I'm thinking, Vanderburgh Electronics may well be the largest in the state with Tamarac second. I don't like that position. Never have, but until now, I haven't been in the position to do anything about it. I want to buy Vanderburgh. Wait before either of you say anything. I'm not crazy. Here's what I want to happen. Harold, have the will read soon. You know what's in it. I don't want to know anything about it until it's public knowledge. Then I want to know everything.

"Winton, I want you to scour the public records looking for any and all documents you can find that might be useful. I want you to approach the Vanderburghs to see what their price might be if they're willing to sell. Ask that idiot Vivian. Tell them you have a potential buyer. Harold, go over my entire portfolio and tell me what I'm worth. Don't sugarcoat it either of you. Now let's eat and discuss it."

Harold was the first to chime in. "Tamara, you know I love you like a daughter, but I don't think I can do this for you. I don't know much about the will. Bob amended it and gave it to me in a sealed envelope with the instructions not to open it until all the family was together for the reading. As you know, until the will has been read, I can't discuss it. You understand this has nothing to do with you. Well, I guess it does have something to do with you after all. What I meant to say is you personally with me."

"Tamara, are you sure you want to fight a privately held

company as large as Vanderburgh?" Winston asked. "Can't you buy up some smaller ones first and get the feeling for running a bigger corporation? Do you realize that the family wholly owns Vanderburgh's stock?"

"First, Harold, thanks for being so candid with me. I expected nothing less. Second, let me see if I can logically and not emotionally answer Winton's questions. Let me begin by asking how big is big. How large is large. It's large only if you're looking at it through jaundiced eyes as if it were an impossible dream. Had I come out of Lawrence with that attitude, I wouldn't have gotten this far in a field dominated by white males. I have higher aspirations than that. I want to be the first black female entrepreneur to succeed in that same world, and how better to do it than to buy up all the competition when it becomes available?

"As far as its being a privately held corporation is concerned, only an idiot in the business wouldn't know that. But look at the family. A woman who wouldn't know her way outside to the car unless someone escorted her; an egotistical, maniacal son who'll run the company into the ground within a year with his extravagance, a beautiful daughter who can't keep her pants on to save her soul, and a drunkard younger son. Do you seriously think these people are capable of running their noses never mind a multimillion-dollar company? I don't think so. Does that answer your question? I've thought about this for a while, and the opportunity has now presented itself. I want to go for it. Make it happen, gentlemen, and you'll end up rich beyond your wildest dreams."

"I told you I didn't think I could help you," Harold said.

"Yes, I know. You alluded to before the will was read. I'm willing to wait until the will is read. Then you could cut ties with the Vanderburghs."

Winton hemmed and hawed around but finally agreed to look into the finances though he said it might take a while.

"Will the will be read by a week from now? Yes? Fine. Winton, you have a week. We'll meet back here then. Now, which of you is paying the tab?"

CHAPTER 7

P oor Madeline. She was way out of her league. She went to her sometimes-physical trainer. Most people knew how he physically trained her.

Meanwhile, Rory crawled back into the Do Drop Inn and poured himself onto a barstool; luckily, he didn't pour off the other side.

"What did my brother want?" Rory was still obviously drunk.

"He wanted you to call him. He said it was an emergency. I was supposed to call him for you if you couldn't do it yourself. If I had to, I was supposed to prop you up."

"I couldn't make a call if I wanted to. Don't have a phone. Don't have a number."

"I have a phone and a number. Your brother told me to call if you couldn't."

"Did he tell you what to do if I didn't want to talk to him?"

"I'm calling him anyway."

The bartender, Johnny, took the phone number from his pocket and dialed it. He waited and waited for the phone on the other end to start ringing. He looked up to see Rory peering at him with a ragged grin and the phone cord circling his head like a lasso.

"Gotta beer? I told you I didn't want to talk to him."

"Put that line back in. I want to talk to your brother even if you don't. He said it was an emergency."

Rory put the cord back in and stumbled out the door.

Johnny dialed again.

"Hello?"

"Yeah, this is Johnny, from the bar. Your brother just ran out of the door because I told him I was going to call you. He's so drunk that you'll probably find him out back asleep by the dumpster if not in it."

"Okay, thanks. Try to keep him there, and don't tell him you called me. I'll be there within an hour. Try to sober him up. I'll pay you for the coffee."

CHAPTER 8

D r. Melvin Blumstein called Detective Sergeant Flores with the forensic findings of the autopsy but refused to give them over the phone.

"I suggest you come down here, Sergeant. You might want to bring your lieutenant with you. I found something very interesting."

"Why don't you just tell me now and save me a trip all the way across town?"

"Because what I found is very interesting. Just come down and bring the lieutenant with."

"All right, we'll be there soon."

Flores went to get the lieutenant.

"Hey Lieutenant, Blumstein called. He's completed the autopsy on Vanderburgh."

"Let me see it. I'll bet there's no evidence of foul play."

"He wouldn't give it to me over the phone. He said it was too big to fax. He wants us to come down there because he found something very interesting, he said."

"What was it? And what was so interesting about it that he couldn't tell you over the phone?"

"I don't know, sir. He wouldn't say. He was adamant that I should bring you down there with me right away."

On the way down to the morgue, the lieutenant said, "I'll bet it was poisoning after all. We have a murder on our hands."

"No, I'll bet the notorious teetotaler has cirrhosis of the liver."

"Nah. It's nothing at all, just a bad ticker."

Flores turned into the morgue driveway and parked in the police-assigned area. Several squad cars from other agencies were there. It looked like business was good in the autopsy department. Other than autopsies, the morgue was also the repository for the unknowns, the John and Jane Does. It's pretty bad when the storage areas gets so full that the morgue has to start turning corpses away.

The sergeant and lieutenant went to Dr. Blumenstein's office on the first floor. His secretary had to call him from the autopsy theater to meet the cops.

He came up, poked his head into the office, and beckoned them to follow him. They descended to the netherlands of pathologic science.

Vanderburgh's body was draped modestly with a sheet splotched with blood as was the doctor's gown. The doctor threw back the sheet with a flourish. "What do you make of that?" he asked pointing.

The policemen saw nothing except a gaping chest with organs in it. The doctor started to show them things they wouldn't have known. "Look at this, the liver. Do you see the discoloration? That indicates it had degenerated significantly."

The sergeant nudged the lieutenant. "See, Lieutenant? I told you it was cirrhosis."

"Not quite, Sergeant. See these? The kidneys. They too had degenerated substantially. Interesting, no? This is the heart. Look at the amount it has withered. It looks like the heart of a ninety-year-old man. This gentleman was poisoned. The probable source is from Amanita mushrooms. They're abundant in America and Europe. They can easily be mistaken for good mushrooms and ingested.

"They can be used to make tea, coffee, or sautéed and eaten over steak. Since there are no immediate signs or symptoms, the victim can even eat an entire mushroom and not know anything is wrong and thus not seek medical attention until it's too late. Whether these mushrooms were ingested intentionally or not is speculative. I couldn't say with any certainty if this death was a homicide or not. All I can say is that he was poisoned. I'd treat this as a homicide at this juncture."

CHAPTER 9

Flores, the head detective on the case, had no clues or evidence. There was no sign of a break-in, no signs of a struggle. The CSI team had finished with their fingerprinting, photographing, and vacuuming for trace evidence but had found nothing unusual or unexpected.

Flores waited until they were finished. He began to look in corners, in drawers, on bookshelves. He even looked behind the books but came up with nothing. He stroked his beard pondering how this could have been a murder.

Puzzled, he went to Vanderburgh's favorite restaurant to find out what he had eaten in the past few days. Flores asked to see the head chef.

The chef came out of the kitchen wiping his hands on his apron. He looked at Flores surprised and curious. "Hello, Sergeant Flores. What brings you here?" Flores was a frequent guest at the restaurant.

"Hello, Chef Stevens. I was hoping you could help me out with an investigation I'm working on."

"I'd be happy to if I can. What would you like to know?"

"You hear about the death of Robert Vanderburgh? The coroner thinks it might have been a murder from ingesting some exotic mushrooms. I'd like to know what Vanderburgh had to eat in the past couple of days."

"You're not implying I had anything to do with it, are you?

I'll have you know I run a very efficient and clean kitchen. I go through thousands of mushrooms a week, but I assure you they're the best quality. They aren't poisonous."

"No, Chef, I'm not implying anything. I need to know what he had to eat."

"Uh ... Let's see. Tuesday was beef tips with mushrooms. Wednesday was an omelet—cheese, ham, and mushrooms. Thursday, it was veal-parm with mushrooms, and yesterday, he had a Philly cheese steak minus the green peppers."

"I see. There seems to be a theme here. Is there any way for someone to slip in some of those exotic mushrooms?"

"I suppose so, but it would have to happen outside my kitchen, though. I or any of my sous chefs would have noticed foreign mushrooms. We use only button tops, shiitake, and portabellas. These exotic mushrooms must look different."

"Okay, but could I see the batch you have now?"

"I don't like outside people in my kitchen. Why don't you trust me?"

"Because I'm naturally suspicious. It's not that I don't trust you. I'm working on a possible homicide using mushrooms. I need to look at all the possibilities. That includes your kitchen."

"I still don't like it. I'm sure that there's nothing wrong with my mushrooms."

"If you prefer, I can get a search warrant."

"Since you put it that way, come with me."

They walked into the kitchen. Flores was impressed by the amount of chaotic activity. It was noisy, hot, and steamy. Chefs were hurrying everywhere. Servers scurried in and out. Everything was controlled pandemonium. He and the chef went to the walk-in refrigerator. Flores was surprised to see box after box of fresh mushrooms—button tops, shiitakes, and portabellas. He immediately saw the big differences between the three varieties and understood what the chef had meant about his and his crew spotting any other variety of mushrooms right away.

"I think I can put away the suspicion that you might have had those exotic mushrooms somehow in your kitchen. I apologize."

"I told you, Sergeant, but no offense taken. How about I cook you something on the house?"

"No. I appreciate it, but I'm on duty. I have to prove this thing with Vanderburgh was or wasn't a murder."

CHAPTER 10

H arold called Vivian to have the family come in for the will reading the following day. The funeral had been put off until the police released the body, but the will could be read.

Vivian immediately called Robert. "Have you found your brother yet? Where is he? The will can't be read until he's there and sober enough to understand how much he isn't getting."

"No, Mother, I haven't found him yet, but I have a lead on him."

"Follow that lead until it drops you into the Detroit River or Lake Michigan whichever direction it takes you. Do *not* come back without him. The reading is scheduled for tomorrow."

"Yes ma'am."

Vivian called Madeline only to get her voice mail. She left a message: "Get out of bed with that supposed trainer of yours and call your mother right now."

Vivian sat and worried. Her children needed to be there for her to find out what changes had been made and how they would affect her.

The phone rang. Vivian picked up on the first ring.

"Hello, Mother. How did you know where I was?"

"It's not hard. Everyone knows about your escapades. The will reading is going to be tomorrow. I want you here by eight in the morning. No going out on your husband, and no late-night sex with him. I want you on time. It's important."

"Yes, Mother."

Robert finally caught up to his brother in the Do Drop Inn. Rory was living up to his reputation. He was drunk and flirting with the whores who frequented the bar. How he got money for his drinks was a big mystery.

"Rory! Rory!" Robert practically shouted. "Rory, you have to come with me now! Mother wants you in Canton right away."

"What's the matter, big brother? Did she slip off her broomstick again? Can't you help her up yourself?"

"No, you lush. Father died. The will reading is tomorrow."

Rory sobered up in a big hurry. "Wha ... What did you say? Dad died? How? When? And what will?"

"Apparently, he had a heart attack at his desk. The police and the coroner are investigating as if it were a homicide, but it sure looked like a heart attack to me. Come with me. I'll get you cleaned up and dressed properly and keep you sober. I might even get some decent food in you. When was the last time you ate anyway?"

"I don't know. A couple of days ago, I think. It doesn't matter. I don't get hungry."

"Of course not. Your belly is full of booze all the time. Where do you get your money? No, I don't want to know."

They left in Robert's black Cadillac Escalade. On the way back to Canton, Rory slept and snored. Robert was hoping he could have talked to his little brother for a while.

Madeline was reluctant, but she made her trainer get up and go home. Then she started a warm bubble bath. She placed scented candles all around the tub, got a glass of red wine, got in, lay back, and drifted off to sleep. She was there when her husband got home from work.

"Madeline!" Harry shouted. "Madeline! Where are you? Where's dinner?"

Madeline stirred in the cold bathwater, stood and showered, and called down to Harry, "I'm in the bath. We can go out for dinner or have something delivered. I didn't feel like cooking."

Harry thought that was happening more frequently. At least three times a week and sometimes on the weekend, Madeline didn't feel like cooking. He still didn't have a clue about the real reason she didn't want to cook—her afternoon trysts.

"By the way, Harry, Mother called this afternoon. The will reading is tomorrow morning. She wants us there early. I don't know if Robert has found Rory yet. He has to be there for the will to be read."

"Really? I have a court appearance tomorrow morning. Can't it be postponed until afternoon?"

"You know Mother."

"Yes, I do. She always gets her way. Well, I have the appearance tomorrow, so I can't make it."

"Can't you get a continuance or whatever you lawyers call them? Mother will be furious if you're not there and it holds up the reading."

"No, I can't. It's a nasty divorce with custody battles and financial considerations. I really need to be there."

"I'll bet Mother could get you the continuance if you'd let her. Who's the judge?"

"Henry Potter. She probably could, but I don't want her to. It's probably too late now anyway."

"Get ready for dinner, but first, tell me if you want to stay in or go out."

"I'd rather stay in. I'm bushed. I think I'll take a shower while we wait. Why don't you order Chinese? I want a large Singapore noodle."

"Okay."

They ate in front of the TV that night and went to bed early. Madeline wanted just to sleep, but Harry had other ideas.

CHAPTER 11

In the morning, they all gathered in Harold's office for the reading of the will. Harold, always the considerate host, offered everyone coffee, water, or tea. Robert asked for coffee black with no sugar, Madeline declined anything, and Vivian wanted Earl Grey tea. Rory piped in, "I want a beer."

Harold replied, "Not now, Rory. I'm going to read the will."

Robert was incensed. "For Pete's sake, Rory, can't you skip one once in a while?"

"Who is Pete?" asked Rory.

Right then, a handsome young attorney walked in with a sheaf of paper for Harold, grinned mischievously at Vivian, turned, and walked out.

Wow, Vivian thought. So did Madeline.

Vivian asked, "Harold, who was that?"

Madeline was wondering the same thing. She started to plot how she could get him to pay attention to her.

Harold said, "My new associate, Jason Plummer. He just passed the bar exam. I think he'll be an exceptional attorney. Shall we get comfortable? This could take a while."

He took his time cleaning his reading glasses; he wanted to stall for time. He had a feeling that this was not going to be a pleasant reading of a will. He picked up the papers that Jason had brought in, cleared his throat, and began to read.

"The last will and testament of Robert J. Vanderburgh Sr. I,

Robert J. Vanderburgh Sr., being of sound mind, declare this to be my last will and testament. It supersedes all others. Being of sound mind, Mr. Attorney, I want to dispense with all the legalities and make this as easy to read and understand that even you, Mr. Attorney, will abide by it.

"First, to my worthless, lying, cheating wife, Vivian Vanderburgh, I give the house in Saint Clair Shores, Michigan. She can also have all her jewelry and whatever cash is in our checking account. The household expenses will be paid from the trust fund I set up for that purpose. If she uses it all up, too bad. The household staff will also be paid from this fund for however long it lasts.

"Second, to my lazy, conniving, plotting, snake-in-the-grass son, Robert J. Vanderburgh Jr., I leave my Ping golf clubs so he can claim to have been better than me playing golf. He can also have the house he has been living in rent free. However, he will have to take over the real estate taxes and the other household expenses.

"Third, to my whore of a daughter, Madeline Grath, and her equally sleazy husband, I leave nothing except the trust fund that has already been set up. I hope that this will make them get out of whatever bed they happen to be sleeping in at this moment and find suitable jobs to support their extravagant lifestyles.

"Last, to my drunkard son, Rory Vanderburgh, I leave nothing. He would only sell it to buy drugs or booze. I desire that he seek help for his addictions. In the off chance that he does, I am setting aside money in a trust fund to be used only for his rehabilitation. If he passes away before using this gift, it will all go to my church.

"That does it for the family. Now for the business. I would like to decrease the shares held by the family, but I am told by Mr. Attorney that I can't. So I will divide up what I can. I own seventy-nine percent of the company with the rest equally distributed to my worthless offspring each holding seven percent.

"To my loyal, longtime secretary, friend, and sometimes

confidant, Clara Barton, I give fifty-one percent of the company to be run as she sees fit. No one is better able to take over the reins. She has been privy to all my desires and dealings and how I ran the company.

"The remaining twenty-eight percent will go to my head of security, Tom Davis, also a longtime friend and loyal to the core.

"I don't doubt that this will will be contested, that there will be dissension in the ranks, and that backstabbing will occur between my children. I have every confidence that Clara will take care of everything in good order. Signed, Robert J. Vanderburgh Sr."

There was a stunned silence for a minute while that sunk in. Then there was pandemonium when everyone started talking or rather yelling at once.

"This can't be! I'll get another attorney to contest this! This is a travesty! How could the old man do this to me?" roared Robert.

"To you? What about me? He called me a whore!" yelled Madeline.

Rory sarcastically said, "We all know you're a whore. So what if the old man called you one?" He was laughing so hard that he nearly peed his pants.

Vivian sat in stunned silence. She didn't know for once what to do or how to react to this surprising news.

All the family members except Rory stormed out of Harold's office; Rory was rolling around on the floor laughing.

Jason, who had heard all the shouting, sat on the corner of the secretary's desk with one long leg dangling and the other one planted firmly on the floor.

Touching Vivian's elbow ever so slightly as she passed, he asked, "Mrs. Vanderburgh? I'm sorry about your misfortune. I couldn't help but hear."

She glanced at him and noted his baby-blue eyes, strong chin, gleaming smile, and broad chest. She paused. Her breath quickened.

"Yes?"

"I was wondering if you might like to get a cup of coffee or something."

"I don't know. After all, my husband just died and cheated me out of my money."

"I know all that, ma'am. I thought you could use some company."

"Yes, I suppose I could use some company away from the family to sort out what just happened and to think about what to do next."

"Great! Let me tell the boss I'll be out of the office for a while."

CHAPTER 12

They went out of the building, stepped into her limousine, and got comfortable in the back seat. While they were riding to a coffee shop, they didn't talk much. Their legs, however, were very close together, almost touching.

Vivian felt the heat from Jason's leg. She also felt the temperature rising in her body. She was a little flustered because that hadn't happened in a long time. She felt a little uncomfortable. She didn't know what was happening or what to do about it.

They found a booth toward the back of the shop. Vivian slid in first. Jason slipped in next to her. Their knees touched briefly. Sparks flew through Vivian's body. She flushed with embarrassment at her reaction to the fleeting touch, but Jason didn't seem to notice.

After they ordered coffee, there was an awkward silence that Jason finally broke.

"Vivian? May I call you Vivian? What are you going to do next?"

"Yes, you may. I don't know. I suppose I'll live in the house. The money in the trust and our bank accounts should be enough for now. I would have been a lot better off if Robert had given me the company."

"How so seeing that you don't know how the business runs and have never worked at anything?"

"I could have sold it. I hear that Tamara Hayes is interested in it. I could have let Robert run it, or I could have let Clara, his secretary, run it."

"Yeah, I suppose so, but that is moot now. Clara will probably build the business up because she knows what your husband was thinking."

The waitress brought the coffee and asked if there was anything else she could get for them. Jason told her no, that they were all right.

"May I suggest that you have someone look into investing some of your money for you? That way, your money would last longer."

"That's a good idea. Do you know anyone?" asked Vivian.

"Sure. I could do it for you."

"You? I didn't know you knew anything about investing."

"I'm an attorney, yes, but I know some of the ins and outs of investing because I handle my own money. I don't want to work for Harold for the rest of my life. I want to go out on my own someday soon."

Jason reached over, put his fingertips lightly on Vivian's delicate hand, and looked into her eyes. "Vivian, I want you to know that I care about you and don't want you hurt or wanting for anything."

Stunned, Vivian asked, "How can you? I only just met you. You know nothing about me."

"Simple. I asked Harold about you. I saw your interactions with Robert Sr. at his office. I knew you were not happy about the way he treated you. I longed to meet you. Now that I have, I must say that I'm very impressed and frankly quite smitten by you."

"Jason," she said quietly, "how can you be? I must have thirty years on you. I have three grown children. I'm an old woman."

"I don't agree. You're not old; you're experienced. Besides, I'm only twenty years younger. Do you see? I know a lot more than you think."

"Uh, yeah. I think it's about time I go."

Jason walked Vivian out to the limo, opened the door, and made sure she was snuggled in. He peered in and said, "Call me. Or may I call you?"

"Umm. I'll call you. Goodbye, Jason."

He closed the door and watched the limo move away from the curb and head down the street.

CHAPTER 13

"Tamara, this is Harold. I'm calling with what I've found out about Vanderburgh Electronics. I read the will today to the family. It seems that the old man really stuck it to his family. No one gets what amounts to anything. He left fifty-one percent of the company to his secretary, Clara Barton, and twenty-eight percent to Tom Davis."

"What?" Tamara exclaimed. "That must have created quite a stir. What did they do?"

"They screamed of course. It effectively cuts the whole family out of running the company. Each of the kids has only seven percent. If a fight were to come up, they would have only a combined twenty-one percent, not enough to mount a hostile takeover."

Tamara thought about it for a few minutes and then said, "Okay, here's what I want you to do. Call Clara and offer her twenty-six point five million for her shares. Then call Davis and offer him one point four million for his. Let's see how hungry they are."

Harold was shocked. "Why, that's only half a million for each share. The stock is probably worth a million or more each." Harold came up with those figures approximating what the offer was divided by the percentage each got.

"I know. That's the beauty of it. Either I can get them for cheap or at least find out if they're interested in selling. That's just a start. I intend to buy Vanderburgh Electronics."

CHAPTER 14

Vivian went straight home after coffee with Jason and went to her bedroom without stopping to see if the staff was still working; she wasn't worried about dinner. What she was concerned about was her date with Jason. She didn't know what to feel about an innocent cup of coffee. She didn't know why the light touch of his hand on hers had affected her so much. In her mind, the spot still burned with a passionate fire.

I'm quite a bit older than Jason, but why should that matter? she asked herself. *Plenty of older men have younger girlfriends or wives. Am I not entitled to some warmth and comfort in my older years? I'm still an attractive woman. Evidently Jason thinks so.*

With shaking hands and butterflies in her stomach, she reached for the phone. She would call Harold's office about the will and find out if Jason was back yet; maybe she could find out more about him.

"Harold, this is Vivian. I want to ask some questions about the will."

"What would you like to know?"

"Have you checked to see if it's in his handwriting? Can it be voided? Is it a fake?"

"Whoa! Slow down. Let's take one question at a time. I know that Robert wrote the will in his own hand. Jason witnessed his signing it, so his signature is real. I don't think there's a very good chance that it can be voided. Lots of people write their wills."

"Hmmm. Is there anything we can do to stop Clara from taking over?"

"No, Vivian, there isn't."

"Okay. I think we'll just have to live with it for now. By the way, is Jason back?"

"What do you mean for now? Please forget about it. And yes, I think he is. Would you like to talk to him?"

"Heavens no! Why on earth would I want to talk with him?"

"I saw you two leave together this morning."

"Yes, we left together. We went for some coffee. Jason thought I could use a little companionship."

"He's right. You probably could use someone to lean on in this difficult time. I'm not sure he's the one, though."

"Why not? He's young, handsome, and smart, and he seems to genuinely care about what happened to me today."

"Yes, I'm sure he is, but beware. I think he may be after your money."

"Do you think he's that type? Why did you hire him?"

"For the same reasons you might be attracted to him. He's smart, handsome, and young. But most of all, he has the ambition to make lots of money."

"That doesn't make him a bad person. Thanks for the warning and the answers to my questions about the will. I'll talk to you later."

"Wait a minute."

She heard silence and static as Harold put her on hold. Soon, she heard a deep voice.

"Hello. This is Jason. How may I be of assistance to you?"

"This is Vivian. I must have been rerouted to the wrong phone."

"No, I don't think so. Harold rang me before he transferred the call. It's so good to hear your voice again. What's up? How can I help you?"

"I don't know. Maybe we can get together to talk about

investing. Or maybe we can discuss the provisions of the will. Do you think there's any way to break it?"

"That would be a good idea. I would like to see your wealth grow. But I don't think there's anything we can do to break the will. Did Harold tell you that I had witnessed the signing?"

"Yeah, he did. What does that mean?"

"Look, I don't want to discuss it on the phone. Why don't I come over tonight? We could go to Izakaya Sanpei for dinner. They serve great sushi."

"All right. Do I have to bring anything? Like my bank statements?"

"No, we'll get to that soon enough. Pick you up at seven?"

"Okay. Do you know where I live?"

"Yes. See you at seven."

CHAPTER 15

Detective Sergeant Flores was at his desk pondering the situation. He was no further with the investigation of Vanderburgh's murder and was wondering what to do next besides reinterview everyone involved, but he still had questions. *Whom to start with? What questions to ask? How can I sniff out the liar or liars if there are any?*

He would have to research sources for Amanita mushrooms, find out who had recently bought some, and determine if there were any legitimate uses for them.

He googled Amanita mushrooms; to his dismay, he learned that *Amanita muscaria* grew readily in Michigan and in particular the Upper Peninsula mostly at the edges of woods. He discovered that they were edible but with caution. They contained muscimol, which produced euphoria, hallucinations, muscle spasms, drowsiness, sweating, pupil dilation, and increased body temperature.

Flores thought it was interesting that they could be eaten, that they were considered poisonous but rarely caused death. They had been used in religious rites by people in Siberia for years. The side effects of consumption were hallucinations and muscle spasms, but they lasted only a few hours. There was no evidence that they damaged the liver or kidneys.

Now what? He went over the facts. Vanderburgh was dead, presumably murdered. He had liver damage and kidney disease.

Robert Jr. was broke. Clara was at that point a rich woman. Tom Davis no longer needed to work. *How would each benefit from Vanderburgh's death?*

Neither Tom nor Clara looked like they needed anything. They had good salaries and were steady workers at Vanderburgh Electronics. They didn't expect to gain anything from Vanderburgh's death. Everyone seemed to be surprised when the will was read.

Robert needed money for certain. He had thought he was a shoo-in for the head of the company. He stood to make millions. Rory was a deadbeat. All he cared about was his booze and a place to sleep. Madeline had no cares as long as Daddy's allowance kept coming in. She didn't have a mind for money as long as she had her personal trainers.

What about Vivian? She was shrewd, Flores thought, wise in the ways of the world. She would have significantly benefitted but would probably sell the company because she had no desire to run the business, and she didn't trust Robert to run it for her. Besides Clara, she had had the closest contact with Robert Sr.

How about Tamara Hayes? Vanderburgh's biggest competitor. She could gain if the company went under. Or could she buy it now?

CHAPTER 16

Tired from scurrying around trying to finalize arrangements for the funeral dinner, Madeline fell exhausted into the arms of her personal trainer. She didn't know what else to do. She thought he might be able to help her. But he had different ideas and priorities.

"Calm down, Madeline. It's going to be all right. All we have to do is make love to get your mind off of the funeral."

"How can you think about that at a time like this? I lost my allowance from Daddy. I don't have much of the company. No source of money. I'll lose everything."

"What a great opportunity! You're independent of the family. They no longer control you. You're a free woman."

"What do you mean independent? I still have a husband and no money of my own."

"You're free from the Vanderburghs' control. You can do what you want. That idiot of a husband of yours would gladly finance your heart's desire."

"Maybe you're right," Madeline said as she began to relax in his arms. "Let's sleep on it. It'll be clearer in the morning."

"I had other ideas."

"Down boy, I'm tired and want to sleep. G'night." She went home, took a bath, and went straight to bed.

CHAPTER 17

R ory finally controlled his laughter. He hitched a ride to his favorite hangout, the Do Drop Inn. Since he had no money, he was hoping that someone would buy him a drink. After the morning, he was parched but still buzzed.

"Hey everyone! Guess what happened at the reading of the will? The old man cut everyone out of the will. He gave everything to his secretary and a private cop. Ain't that a riot?"

Johnny, the bartender, asked, "So that means you got no money. That's no surprise. You never have any anyway."

"Yeah, but that's okay 'cause I get along without it. As long as people buy me drinks, as long as there's Sheila."

"You still sponging off that old whore? She's so ugly her mother thought she was the afterbirth."

"Gimme a drink, will you, Johnny?"

"Just one. Then you'll have to mooch off someone else."

"Okay. Gimme a double Jim Beam on the rocks."

"Pushing it, aren't you, Rory? You usually get a beer."

"Yeah. You said only one, so I figured I'd get something with a real kick. I need a boost after this morning."

Johnny poured the drink not skimping on the booze. It was more like four shots than two. Lots of ice of course.

Rory was sipping his bourbon and scoping out the patrons to assess whether he could finagle a drink from one of them. He peered through the darkness and finally settled on his next victim.

A moment later, the door opened, and a woman entered the place. She sauntered up to the bar self-confidently and sat on a stool next to Rory. She took her sunglasses off revealing gorgeous baby-blue eyes. She smiled at Rory and asked Johnny for a drink. She was good looking, but she looked like she had had a hard life. Her blond hair reached almost to her waist. She had lines around her eyes, and her lips were pursed with the telltale signs of smoking. She once could have been very attractive, but her hard life had stolen that. She was still shapely but in a downtrodden way.

She turned to Rory, flashed a smile, and asked, "Hi, handsome. What's your name?"

In his drunken state, Rory thought she looked terrific. "Ro— Rory," he stammered.

"That's a cute name. It suits you. You want a drink?"

"Sure! I never turn down the chance to have a drink with a lovely lady. Wait, you're not a whore or something, are you?"

"No darling, I'm not. I'm here because I got lonely and thirsty. What are you having?"

"Jim Beam. Make it a double."

"Hey barkeep, pour my friend a double Jim Beam straight up."

"Okay, ma'am, but he's drinking well bourbon on the rocks."

"That's all right. Give him what he wants."

Johnny brought Rory his drink. Casually wiping the bar, he stayed within earshot; he was curious to learn more about this mysterious woman.

The woman smiled again at Rory. "You're a regular here, aren't you? I think I've seen you before. You look very familiar. Do you live near here?"

"You sure ask a lot of questions, don't you? Yes, I'm a regular. I come here as often as I can, which is pretty much every day. No, I don't live nearby. I crash wherever I can." Rory peered at her. "Do you have a name? You look vaguely familiar."

"Sure, silly. Everyone has a name. Mine happens to be Veronica, but you can call me Ronnie. My last name is Vanderburgh."

Rory nearly fell off his stool. Johnny dropped the glass he was polishing. Both gasped.

"Wait! What did you say? Vanderburgh?"

Johnny wanted to know, "Is this some kind of cruel joke?"

"No, it's not a joke. I could show you my driver's license. What does it matter anyway? Have you heard the name before?"

"My last name's Vanderburgh too," Rory blurted out.

"Rory's old man just passed away. He owned Vanderburgh Electronics. Are you one of those long-lost relatives who come crawling out of the woodwork when someone wealthy dies?"

"No, but let's slow down a bit. You said his father died. As far as I know, mine's alive and well. He's rich, but I don't know what he does. His plant is in Livonia I think."

"That sure is a coincidence. Rory's father's place is also in Livonia."

"What did you say his first name was?"

"I didn't. It's Robert."

Veronica burst into hysterical tears. "My father's name is Robert too. Could they be the same person?"

CHAPTER 18

Across town, Robert was plotting to dump Clara and Tom on the street. He didn't know how since he, his brother, and his sister controlled a combined 21 percent of the company. He was deathly afraid of Tom and would avoid him at all costs, but he thought he might be able to dig up some dirt on Clara and blackmail her into giving up her controlling shares. He would dig deep into Clara's life, but he would need financing to do that. *I know. I'll enlist Tamara Hayes's assistance. She wants the company as much as I do. She has the money I need.*

He called her.

"Hello, Mr. Vanderburgh. To what do I owe this pleasure?" Tamara breathed into the phone.

"I have a proposition to discuss with you. What it concerns is extremely confidential. Too sensitive for the phone. You never know who's listening."

"Okay. Where do you suggest we meet?"

"Isn't there a Coney Island around the corner from your office?"

"I believe so. I think its name is Thomas. We could meet there. Say around one?"

"That sounds fine. See you then and there."

CHAPTER 19

M adeline finally dragged herself away from her trainer and
made herself presentable. She called a caterer who owed her a
favor, and she got him to agree to cater the funeral dinner at her
house for three times the regular rate.

Exhausted, she had to get the maids to clean the house. She
wanted everything perfect to please her mother. She was so tired
from all the work that she decided to take a well-deserved nap.

CHAPTER 20

J ason sat in his office nervously staring at the phone wondering
whether he should call Vivian. He thought he might be falling
for her. She was so charming especially after just losing her
husband of so many years. He knew it was wrong. He couldn't
help himself. He didn't know if she felt the same. He didn't want
to push himself on her and risk pushing her away.

Growling in anguish, he picked up some briefs he had been
working on, but his mind wandered. All he saw was her beautiful
face. He couldn't concentrate. He got up and started pacing.
Picking up his coffee cup, he strode out to the coffee machine.
He hoped a cup of strong coffee would settle him down. He felt
like a horny teenager with raging hormones.

What's wrong with me? he wondered. *What's wrong with being
attracted to a very pretty woman no matter what the age difference?
After all, plenty of men her age had much younger wives or girlfriends
and no one thought a thing about it. Why the stigma of an older woman
with a younger man?*

When he got back to his desk, he saw the missed call light
flashing. *Could it have been her? No, it was probably a client. Maybe
it was her. Did she leave a message? Probably not. It was just a client.
If it's essential, they'd leave a message or call back. Should I check my
messages?*

He called voice mail and heard, "You have two new messages.
Press one to hear your messages." He hesitated before pressing

one. "Your first new message is from Harold Peabody. Press one to hear the message, two to save, three to skip to the next message."

Jason pressed three. "Your next message is from Vivian Vanderburgh. Press one to hear the message." He immediately pressed one.

"Hello, Jason. This is Vivian. Would you please call as soon as you can? I need to talk to you."

That was it. Nothing further. Nothing hinted. He played the message again to be sure he had heard it all. He had. He picked up the receiver, punched in the numbers, and waited anxiously. One ring. Two. Three. Four. Five. *Maybe she's not going to pick up.* Six. Seven … "Hello? This is Vivian," she said breathlessly. "Jason?"

"Hello, Viv. Can I call you Viv? How can I help you?"

"I'd like it if you did call me Viv. It's a pet name no one uses anymore. It'll be our special name. I need some advice on financial matters. I have a couple of million dollars I'd like to invest, but I have no idea what I should invest in. You said the other day that you could help me. Is that true? I'll pay you of course."

Jason was a bit deflated by the conversation. He had been hoping for something more intimate, like dinner. "Sure I can help. What's your goal? Do you have anything in mind?"

"That's why I need you. I don't know anything at all about investing. I've heard that real estate is good."

"That's true if you don't want to make money quickly. May I suggest we get together to go over your finances and map out a strategy?"

"That sounds fine. Would you like to come over here? I can have Maria put on some of her famous delicious tamales. Would that be all right?"

Jason's heart did a flip-flop. She had asked him to come to dinner. "Yeah, that would be great! What time?"

"We'll have dinner around seven, but come as early as you want. We can go over my finances first."

"Great! See you in about an hour."

He went home to shower, shave, and change clothes. He wanted to look tiptop for her. He was whistling as he got ready.

He arrived at Vivian's house about thirty minutes later, and Vivian answered the door. She stepped back to let him in, closed the door, and reached up to hug him. She squeezed him. He smelled a hint of vanilla. It took his breath away. "Wow! Do you greet everyone that way or just your gentlemen callers?"

"Nope, just you. Please come in."

They went into the library. Besides being filled with first editions, the room was furnished eloquently with plush, comfortable chairs, end tables, and Persian rugs. The chairs had reading lights controlled by remotes. The windows were draped with heavy dark blue velvet. No pictures anywhere. No TV. No stereo. Nothing to distract one from reading or writing. Jason looked around appreciatively thinking that he could spend a lot of time in that room.

Vivian broke into his thoughts. "Can I get you something to drink? I have a fully stocked bar. Beer? Whiskey? Some wine?"

"Just an unsweetened ice tea if you have that."

"Sure. I'll have Maria brew some."

Jason took the portfolio from Vivian, sat at a desk, and started poring over the figures. He was amazed by the organization of a woman who supposedly knew nothing about financial matters. She had all the bank statements in order, the CD numbers, her mutual funds—everything. He muttered, fretted, and calculated. Finally, he calculated that she had just short of $3.9 million in her CDs and mutual funds. She had nearly another million in savings and checking accounts. Plus the household budget of approximately $10,000 a month. She indeed was a rich woman.

Vivian leaned over his shoulder as he was finishing up. He smelled her fresh skin and vanilla perfume. It drove him crazy. He had to move away. He stood and paced the room for a few moments to gather his thoughts. When he returned to the desk, Vivian was looking concerned.

"I have good news and bad. First, you're a very wealthy woman. You have nearly five million in liquid assets and another one point five million in real estate, my estimate of what this house is worth."

"That's great news. What's the bad?"

"Your mutual funds are stagnant. They're earning you nothing. In fact, they're losing. The first thing I suggest is to cash them in and invest elsewhere. And your CDs have all matured. They need to be changed to CDs or other funds that show more growth. How comfortable are you with a little risk? Remember, the more risk, the more gain or loss."

"Based on what you're telling me, I can probably put the low-risk stuff into higher risk. I want to keep a substantial amount liquid, Jason."

"That makes sense. When do you want to get started?"

"The sooner the better I should think."

"Right. We can start tomorrow by cashing in the mutual funds and converting the CDs."

Maria poked her head in the door and announced that dinner was ready in the dining room.

"Okay, Maria. We'll be there directly."

After a wonderful, authentic Mexican dinner with all the fixings, they returned to the library to have after-dinner drinks, cognac for her and iced tea for him. They sat close together on the plush love seat. Their legs barely touched sending chills of anticipation through them.

Jason touched Vivian's chin, gently pulled her closer, and brushed his lips against hers. She did not pull away; she sunk further into the love seat and melted into his embrace. They sat there for a long time not moving, not talking, just savoring the moment.

Vivian moved even closer to Jason if that were possible, turned her face back to his, and licked her lips, which were begging to be kissed again. Jason responded with a deep kiss; he savored every curve and taste of her mouth, exploring, probing deep into her mouth.

CHAPTER 21

Sergeant Flores, still suspicious about Vanderburgh's death, returned to Vanderburgh's office to see if anything jumped out at him. He gazed around the room letting his mind wander. His eyes roved from wall to wall, from ceiling to floor and back again. On the credenza, he spotted a coffee brewer. *Strange,* he thought. *There's a full-service coffee system in the break room right around the corner from this office. Maybe he liked his coffee fresh, hot, and convenient.*

Flores opened the lid and peered into where the grounds went. He noticed a pinkish residue clinging to the basket and thought that perhaps the CSI unit had checked the grounds with a chemical. He would have to call to find out. He looked some more and discovered what appeared to be pencil eraser shavings under the brewer. *How could this be? The CSI unit dusted and collected samples. How could they have missed this?*

Flores sat at Vanderburgh's desk, pursed his lips, and steepled his fingers. He was thinking so intently that he didn't hear the door open or see a CSI technician standing there with his mouth gaping wide with surprise.

"Oh hi, Sergeant Flores. I didn't expect to see you here. I came back to finish my investigation. I still have the credenza area to do."

"You haven't finished yet? Why not? This place has been released back to me by your department."

"Yeah, I know, but I told them I wasn't done yet. They told me it would be all right, that I could finish today. There was no hurry since it looks like natural causes."

"We don't know that yet. Wait … You said you hadn't done the credenza yet? So it hasn't been processed yet?"

They went to the credenza. Flores pointed at the shavings. "What do you make of these?"

Following Flores's finger, the technician saw the shavings. "Looks like pencil eraser dust, you know, from erasing something."

"That's what I thought. There's more of the same stuff in the coffee grounds. I want these things analyzed right away."

"Okay, Sarge," the technician said as he gathered samples into evidence bags. "I'll have this done first thing this afternoon."

"I want them done immediately. No stopping for lunch. No flirting with the lab girls. I want them done yesterday!"

The technician walked outside with the specimen samples. As he reached the rear door of his van, the rear window shattered into millions of glass pellets. *Crack!* came the sound of a high-powered rifle. The technician dove for cover behind a wheel. The tire suddenly exploded peppering him with shards of rubber.

Flores had heard the crack of the rifle and ran outside with pistol drawn. *Crack!* Another round was fired. It hit Flores squarely in the chest. He went down in a heap. Silence. Nothing more. The technician had not been injured but was scared. Nonetheless, he crept slowly to Flores, who wasn't moving. Staring at the sergeant, the technician was perplexed. Flores had a gaping hole in his chest, but there was no blood. Flores regained his breath, began to stir, and yelled, "Call for backup! Everyone get down! Don't touch or move anything!"

The technician exclaimed, "Wow! Sarge! You're alive! I thought for sure you were dead!"

"Of course I'm alive you idiot! Thank God for Kevlar! I'm wearing a vest. I'll be okay. A little sore and a bit bruised, but that's better than having a big hole in my chest."

Four squad cars came screeching to a stop in front of Vanderburgh Electronics with sirens blaring and lights flashing. Two more cordoned off each end of the street. Out of each car scrambled two troopers with guns drawn.

Sergeant Flores got up, dusted himself off, and took charge. A trooper told him that he should sit down, that he had this. He was the precinct's lieutenant. "Sergeant Flores, an attempt has been made on your life. You've been shot. Wait for an ambulance. We got this. Tell us what happened."

"Lieutenant, I don't know. I was inside investigating the Vanderburgh death. I heard gunshots and came out to see what was happening and was struck in the chest. It's a good thing I had my vest on. Wait! There was a CSI technician here with evidence he and I found. I need it processed immediately. Is he okay?"

"Yes. He'll be fine. He called in the assault. Can you think of any reason someone would want you dead?"

"No sir unless I'm getting close to something in my investigation."

"Sit and relax as much as you can. We'll talk later."

The lieutenant turned to shout directions and orders to the other patrolmen.

CHAPTER 22

Robert met Tamara at Thomas's restaurant. They found a back booth so they could talk without being overheard. After they ordered coffee, Tamara opened up.

"Okay, Robert, what's going on? I heard that your father died. How does that affect me?"

"Here's the thing. I know you wanted to buy Vanderburgh before the old man passed away. I don't know what you know about the will and what he did to us."

"I know nothing about what's happening."

"The ME and the police are thinking he was murdered. The will was handwritten, so I'm contesting it. The one that was read gave the company to his mistress, Clara Barton, and nothing to Mom. Madeline, Rory, and I retain the seven percent shares we already have but nothing more. That means Clara could get rid of me. I need help … Your help. For me to contest the will, I'll need financing. I thought you might be interested in helping me out a little."

"How much is a little, Robert?"

"All told about a hundred grand to contest the will properly. I can come up with maybe twenty-five thou. I need you to help with the remainder."

"What do I get if I contribute that much?"

"For that, I'll give you fifteen percent of the company. I think that's fair."

"What if I don't?"

"Well then, we'll part as friends with no hard feelings."

"If I'm going to put up that much money, I'll need more. I want fifty-one percent of the company, and I want some assurances that if the will isn't broken, I'll be paid back."

"Don't worry about the money. You'll make substantially more than what you put up. As far as fifty-one percent goes, I can't do that. I have to ensure that I have a majority so that I control the company. I can go up to twenty percent."

"You're asking me to risk seventy-five thousand for a minority share while you're risking only twenty-five thousand? I tell you what. I'll put up all the money for ninety-five percent of the company."

"What? That's highway robbery! Essentially, what you're offering me is the loss of two percent of what I already have."

"Yes, that's right. But look at it this way. You don't have to risk any of your money. And you'll still have a job."

"I *am* risking my money. If the will can't be broken, I'll have to find a way to pay you back."

"I'll let you think about it for a while, or you can come up with another proposal."

CHAPTER 23

B ack at the Do Drop Inn, Veronica caught her breath and started to explain. She said that her mother's name was Clara Barton and that Mr. Vanderburgh was paying for the care of her invalid sister.

Rory realized what had probably happened with Clara and his father. Veronica was the old man's illegitimate daughter. The old man was also paying for the care of Clara's other daughter. Could she also be his? The question then became whether Veronica had any claim on the old man's estate and how that would affect the distribution of the shares of the company.

Veronica asked, "Has the will been read yet? How was the company spit up? Did Mr. Vanderburgh give my mother any money or any shares? What about my sister? Was there anything left to her?"

"The will was read this morning. My brother, sister, and I each got seven percent of the company. He gave your mother fifty-one percent and Tom Davis the remaining twenty-eight percent. There was nothing said about your sister or you for that matter."

"I don't care about myself as long as Mom and my sister are taken care of. That doesn't seem to be the case. With Mom having the controlling interest, she seems to be set. I can't believe this just happened! Apparently, your dad and mine are the same. We're siblings."

"This can't be. It's too weird! My brother, excuse me, our brother is going to go nuts over this not to mention Madeline! Oh, this is just *great!*"

CHAPTER 24

T he police officers who had responded to the shooting found a single rifle cartridge, a 7.62 mm NATO round, meaning that the rifle used was probably an M-14, which had been used extensively in the early years of the Vietnam conflict. It was a powerful and very accurate firearm still preferred by many veterans.

The fact that it was a high-powered rifle was a clue that the UNSUB, the unknown subject, the police were dealing with was someone with military training and possibly a former sniper. It also meant that Flores was probably the target. The other shots were most likely meant to draw Flores out of the building or maybe to scare the CSI technician into dropping the evidence bags compromising the evidence.

The lieutenant was puzzled. *Why would anyone shoot at Sergeant Flores? Was he as he said getting close to the culprit who murdered the senior Vanderburgh? If so, who was it?* "Sergeant Flores, are you up to answering a few questions?"

"Yes sir. I need to get to the bottom of this."

"What you need, Sergeant, is to stand down for a moment. You've been injured in the line of duty. I need you well and thinking straight. Do you know of anyone who'd want you dead? Do you suspect anyone?"

"No sir. As I mentioned, I think I must be close to finding something about Vanderburgh that the UNSUB doesn't want to be known. I can only think that whoever killed Vanderburgh wants the mystery not to unfold."

"Let's go over the facts again. Why were you in Vanderburgh's office? Why was CSI still there? I thought they had released the scene back to the police."

"Yes sir, I did too or I wouldn't have been in there. The CSI technician came back because he hadn't finished collecting evidence. We found some residue in the coffee brewer and under it. He collected it and was going to the lab to have it analyzed right away. He went out with it."

Flores asked, "I'm not dead. I feel okay. When can I resume investigating?"

"Not for a day or so. I want you at full strength. I can't afford to lose you for very long."

"Why not let me go now? I'm fine. I'm just a little sore, and I bet I have a bruise, but that's all. No holes, no blood. I want that guy who took a potshot at me. I want him bad!"

"I don't doubt it, but I need your level head and good mind in the future. I can't afford you to go off half-cocked and hurt somebody especially yourself. I told you when I got here that I had this."

"Are you also cutting me out of the Vanderburgh investigation?"

"No, but I want you to be more careful. Don't go stirring up hornets' nests. Do you have any theories about who did it?"

"Yes sir, but I have no concrete evidence. I suspect that the son did it so he would inherit the company. I know he's having financial difficulties that inheriting the company would solve."

"What about the other family members? Are there siblings who would benefit from their father's death?"

"A younger brother and sister. From what I've found out, the brother is a lush who doesn't care much for the money. The sister is married to a sleazy attorney. I don't know about their financial status. She's said to spend an inordinate amount of money on clothes and jewels."

"I suggest you follow up on the sister's dealings. See if her husband clears enough to pay for her extravagances."

"Yes sir. I do know that they were living in a house owned by the father. I believe they didn't pay anything for it. Same thing with the older son. The younger son was living in a seedy hotel with his girlfriend. His main interest seems to be getting drunk or high. I'll check into them more."

"Great. Tomorrow. Take the rest of the day off. Go home, get drunk or whatever. Don't think about either case. I want you to be fresh in the morning."

"Awww, Lieutenant, I'm fine. I can go to work on it right now."

"No, Sergeant. That's an order. Take the rest of the day off. Don't think about the case."

CHAPTER 25

Clara Barton opened the door to her office thinking that she had so much to do and so little time in which to do it. *What do I do first? Fire Robert? Let him stay on in a lower capacity? I'll have to replace myself. How about production? Should I close the plant for a few days? Will I need to replace Tom now that he has part ownership? Maybe I should talk it over with Tom. He was almost as close to Robert as I was. He might have some insights. Besides, he'll have as much to lose or gain as I do with the decisions I make.*

"Tom Davis, would you please come to my office right away?" she asked over the intercom.

When he heard his name, Tom knew something was up. He rarely if ever had been summoned to the office. He put aside his own investigation of Vanderburgh's death and walked over to the front office. "Hello, Clara. What's up? You look little stressed."

"Hi, Tom. Yes, I am. There are so many things I have to do, and I don't know what to do first. That's why I called you up here. I value your input especially now that you're part owner."

"I'll help you any way I can. Do you want to talk about it here? Perhaps we should go into Robert's office. Is that one of the things you need to do? Decide where your office is going to be?"

"Yes among many other things."

"Clara, I've been thinking about how we can make this place even better. I think the first thing you should do is replace yourself.

Next, move into Robert's office or remodel one. The third would be what to do about Junior."

"See, Tom? That's why I need you. I want you to take over as senior VP of operations. Okay, let's start by replacing you and me. I'll temporarily move into Senior's office so that we can build a new one. Where would you like your office?"

"Near the plant so I can oversee production. What about Junior? What good is he? What can he do?"

"He's good for nothing. All he did was plot how to take over the company. I want to get rid of him, but that might be impossible. He's a good schmoozer. Maybe we can use him in customer relations in a low-key way. What should we do about the plant for the next couple of days? I think it would be a good idea to close down for the weekend and let our people grieve. First thing Monday morning, I'll call a couple of recruiters to get a secretary and a new head of security unless you can think of anyone."

"Okay, that's settled. Let's make Junior director of toilets. No, I guess we can't do that. What can he do without destroying the company? I think he might be fit for the director of maintenance."

"I don't know. That's a lot of responsibility. He's good with numbers, but I don't trust him with the books. How about R&D?"

"What qualifies him for that, Clara?"

"He does have an electrical engineering degree."

"I didn't know that. How do you think he'd get along with the other engineers? They're doing a fantastic job already."

"Yes they are, and I don't want to upset them. All we'd need is a mass exodus to Tamarac."

"We have to put him someplace. How about out to pasture?"

"I wish. Let's think about that one for a while. Let's let our crews go home paid of course, and we should go home too. Monday's going to be one heck of a day."

"I'll let the foremen know. See you Monday."

Tom left wondering if Clara had enough knowledge and experience to run the company.

CHAPTER 26

Rory finally got control of himself. He sobered up quickly with the news that he might have another sister, one no one had known about. He told Ronnie, "We have to go find my brother right now. This changes everything. Do you have a car?"

"Of course I do. It's right outside," answered Ronnie. "Where should we go?"

"First, we go to the plant. Rob is probably in his office. If not, then his home. If he isn't there, he's probably at the country club or his girlfriend's. But first let me finish this drink."

"While you're doing that, I'll go freshen up in the ladies' room."

"I think you look fine. When Robert sees that you've been crying, he'll die."

"Okay. Hurry up."

Rory sipped his drink thinking about how he could break the news to his brother. *Should I call Madeline too? No, she's more than likely with her trainer. What about Mother? No. I'll let Robert handle that. What a mess this is going to be. Correction. Is.*

"What are you thinking about," Ronnie asked. "You look like the cat who swallowed the canary. Is it about how Robert will react to me?"

"You might say that. I hope it gives him a heart attack. Let's get out of here."

They walked out of the bar into the bright sunshine. Her car turned out to be a new, baby-blue Ford Expedition with all the bells and whistles. *Wow!* Rory thought. *This girl must be doing all right for herself. I wonder what she does for a living. If she isn't my sister, maybe I can hook up with her.*

They entered the vehicle. It had plush leather seats and a killer surround-sound system.

"Hey Ronnie, this is a rad car. What do you do for a living?"

"This and that. I'm a consultant for a major fashion shop. I go here and there looking at materials and trends in the marketplace. I also help with designing gowns and dresses that we make. I'm pretty comfortable as you can see."

"Okay, I guess then that you're not one of those, uh, gold diggers looking for riches and sponging off unfortunate people who lost loved ones."

"No I'm not, and I told you I'm not a whore." She laughed. "Where to?"

"Livonia, Stark Road. You can't miss the plant."

They headed for the plant in silence for a while until Ronnie asked, "So what's your story? Why don't you work at the plant?"

"After I got my degree in architectural design, my father told me he didn't need those skills. I tried for months to hawk my skills. The building industry had just suffered a major decline … Nobody hiring. Dear old dad gave me a small but adequate allowance I guess so I wouldn't starve. Instead, I've been trying to drown myself in alcohol. That's gotten me nowhere. Now, I'm the black sheep of the family. If I went into rehab, they might welcome me back, but I'm having too much fun being a thorn in their flesh."

"If you cleaned yourself up, I bet you'd be successful. If you want to get serious and enter rehab, perhaps I can help. I know a few good centers that deal with drugs, alcohol, and some mental illnesses. Would you like me to take you to one?"

"Not right now … Maybe later. This has been such a nightmare. I don't think I could handle it now. How would I pay for it anyway? As you guess, I'm broke."

"Some of these centers don't charge the clients anything. Besides, couldn't you use some of the money that comes from your seven percent of the company?"

"Ya know, I forgot all about that. Until Father died, I couldn't touch it. Maybe I could sell some of it."

"Now that's more like it! Just think about it, okay?"

They arrived at the plant and were surprised to find that it was closed. A guard told them that Clara and Tom had closed it for the weekend. Robert was not on the premises. They would have to look elsewhere.

They headed toward Robert's house, also in Livonia. No Robert. They went to the country club, also no Robert. They went to his girlfriend's house. They found her alone; she hadn't seen him in a couple of days. They were at their wit's end. They had no way of knowing he was meeting with Tamara at that moment.

They went back to the car after confronting Robert's girlfriend. Rory was thinking about what to do next. Ronnie just sat and waited. It was like she had known Rory all her life. She could tell he was deep in thought.

Suddenly, Rory looked up and exclaimed, "Robert gave Johnny his number. Do you have a cell phone? We could call Robert to see where he is."

"I have a phone here. Do you honestly think a girl would go anywhere without one?"

"Good. Do you mind if we go back to the bar to get the number?"

"Why don't I call Johnny? That way, we don't have to go all the way back there."

"Good idea. Do you have the bar's number?"

"Right here on speed dial."

She pressed the button and waited. Johnny answered a moment later. "The Do Drop Inn. This is Johnny."

"Johnny, this is Ronnie. Do you have Robert's cell phone number?"

"Sure. Let me get it for you."

Johnny came back a few moments later. "I'm sorry I had to serve a couple of customers. It's 734-555-7893. Got that? I hope it helps."

"Thanks, Johnny. I do too. Goodbye."

"Bye."

Ronny punched in the numbers, waited for it to ring, and got voice mail. "Robert, this is Veronica. I'm with your brother, and we need to talk to you right away. Please call me using the number on your display." She told Rory, "Now we wait. I hope he'll call soon. What do you want to do in the meantime?"

"How about we get something to eat? I'm starving."

"Good idea. I'm hungry too. Where do you want to go?"

"Thomas's restaurant isn't too far. I hear their food is good."

"Point me in that direction."

They got to the restaurant and were surprised to see Robert sitting with Tamara Hayes in a back corner. Robert and Tamara sat talking conspiratorially and didn't notice Rory and Ronnie as they approached.

"Imagine that. You and Tamara together. What conspiracy are you two talking about?" Rory asked.

"None of your business. What are you doing here? And who is this?"

"This is none other than Veronica Vanderburgh," Rory said with a mischievous grin.

"What did you say? A Vanderburgh? What are you talking about? There are no other Vanderburghs I know of."

"Hello, Robert. Nice to meet you. I'm Veronica Vanderburgh, Clara Barton's daughter. Evidently, my father and yours are the same. I guess he and Mom were having an affair for many years because here I am."

Robert's jaw dropped. "That can't be. If he had been, I would've known about it."

"Maybe. Did you know he was taking care of my invalid sister too? He was paying all the medical expenses. And he sent me to college. All I had to do was maintain a B average."

"This is absurd! I don't believe it. You'll have to prove it. I'll get to the bottom of this, young lady!"

Tamara took it all in. This was the break she needed to get Robert to agree to her proposal.

"All right, miss, what do you want from me? You might as well know that I'm broke, so I couldn't give you anything even if I wanted to. Tamara and I were having a business meeting. Will you excuse us?"

Veronica, taken aback by the venomous response, said calmly, "I don't want anything from you except respect. I don't need your money, nor do I want it. I'm here because I was curious after meeting Rory. I now think I'm here to protect his interests. Remember, I said Dad sent me to school? I went to Wayne State law school. That's right, I'm a lawyer among other things. I now represent Rory, so you can get off your high horse and talk to us. We want to know how my relationship affects the whole situation. It seems to me that you and Ms. Hayes are plotting something. Possibly a buyout or to contest the will. Am I right?"

Robert's ears perked up when he heard her say lawyer. *This could be useful*, he thought. "Okay. So sit down and talk."

CHAPTER 27

T he memorial was held in the chapel of the church the family attended. More people than the chapel could hold showed up—old friends, acquaintances, some enemies, and some curiosity seekers. More were waiting outside to catch a glimpse at the infamous family perhaps.

Robert had been asked to do the eulogy. Nobody else in the family thought that he or she could do it. Vivian and Madeline were basket cases in tears with mascara running; neither could contain herself.

As usual, Rory was drunk. Veronica stood silently looking on. She was a little uncomfortable because she knew she wasn't welcome there. She comforted her mother as best as she could. Tom Davis stood with Clara and Veronica grieving in silence as his friend's casket was wheeled in by the funeral director.

The pastor was the first to speak. "It is my custom whenever there is a funeral to say what amounts to a mini sermon. Today, however, I am going to forgo that because Robert. was a private man and would rather have a celebration rather than a dirge. He loved life and his Lord. He adored his wife of many years and his children, whom he was very proud of. He was beloved by many in the church and the community. He was always giving and cheerful. He will be truly missed. Please say prayers not for Robert but for the family. They are surely grieving and struggling at this sad time. Please join us after the service at Vanderburgh's house for a time of fellowship and food. There will be no interment at this time. I invite Robert to join me in his father's eulogy."

"Thank you, Reverend. Umm, I'm at a loss for words. Did you really know Father, or were you trying to paint a picture of a good man? The man I knew as Father was a good, shrewd businessman. As far as a father was concerned, he was strict, condescending, mean, and self-centered. I suppose he loved us, but he didn't show it very well. We couldn't live up to his standards, or if we did something right, he would change the standards. He would make us clean our rooms every Saturday and then stand by for a white-glove inspection. He almost always found something to complain about.

"I didn't like him very much. I resented that he supported Clara Barton's invalid daughter. He spent more money on that little girl than he did on us. He never went to my baseball games, never encouraged me. He told me I would never amount to anything even after I got my engineering degree.

"He drove my sister into various sexual relationships before she was sixteen. It's a wonder she was able to settle down to one man.

"My brother tried to live up to expectations by going to school and achieving a degree in architectural design with high honors. Father told him not to expect a job at Vanderburgh Electronics. After much searching for a job with no takers, Rory finally gave up. So, dear old Dad drove him to the brink, and he started using drugs and drowning his sorrows with his best friend, Jim Beam.

"For some reason, I'm the only one of us siblings he hired. Although I did well, I felt as though I was nothing more than a gofer. He sent me on one errand after another, schmoosing customers, flying all over the country and outside it too. I think he was trying to keep me away so I couldn't learn the business. That's the true Robert Vanderburgh whom I knew."

Robert went back to his seat. His mother and sister glared at him. Rory sniggered. The was a stunned silence in the sanctuary. The pastor returned to the podium to dismiss the congregation.

"Well, that was certainly a surprise! We have now two pictures of the same man. Please stand while I dismiss you in prayer."

CHAPTER 28

Jason quickly found Vivian. She was seething with anger and pain from her son's words. "Vivian, I had to see how you were feeling after that eulogy. Is there anything I can do?"

"Yeah! You can come home with me and pour me a stiff drink. I can't face all these people. They must think Rob was a tyrant. What got into him, Jason?"

Vivian led Jason to her limo. The chauffeur opened the door for them. She told him to go straight home as fast as he could and not wait for anyone or anything.

Vivian took Jason's hand firmly in hers. Jason was in heaven. He didn't know what to expect next. She was full of surprises.

"After we get rid of the visitors, why don't you stay with me? I promise I won't bite. I need someone to hold and give me comfort."

"Uh, okay, but I don't want to interfere with your mourning."

"Are you kidding? I'm so mad I could chew railroad spikes and spit out nails! I can't believe Robert. How could he demean me in front of all those folks? What was he thinking?"

"Viv, it's obvious he was thinking only of himself. He's upset over the reading of the will and being cut out as he was. When he gets back to work, he'll change his tune."

"That's if he has a job. I heard that Clara was thinking of canning him. Can she do that?"

"I think she can. Rob, in effect, made her the owner of the

company, but to what end? She'll further alienate him and make an enemy. She doesn't need that," Jason reassured her.

"I suppose you're right. But what will she do with him? He expected to become CEO. Now he's out on his ear so to speak, Jason."

"She'll probably use him as Rob did. He'll be her gofer. Can you see the irony in that? He's no better off than he was, and he might be worse."

"Again, I think you're right. How can you be so smart? And handsome too?"

Blushing, Jason retorted, "Aw shucks, ma'am. Ya know, you're a very attractive woman yourself."

"Now Jason, you're going to make me blush. I like it when you're so kind. Please don't think I'm on the rebound. Rob and I haven't been husband and wife for years. I'm feeling a little frisky and free to do what I want. And I want to be with you. I don't want to face the crowd of so-called mourners."

"They're coming to give you support, and some will be trying to comfort you."

"They're coming for a free lunch and gossip. They care nothing about me or what I'm going through," Vivian said venomously. "They want to gawk and be seen. They care nothing for the family or me. They want to see how we lived extravagantly in their minds."

"Oh, I don't know, Viv. I think you're being pretty harsh. A lot of these people are your friends. They do care about you and the family."

"Then why can't they leave me alone and let me grieve in my own way? Can you answer me that? No, I thought not."

"Come on, Viv. You're bitter because you are now a widow, Robert cut you out of the will, and Junior exposed a part of his father that was supposed to remain unknown to the rest of the world. Calm down, fix your makeup, and join me to greet your guests."

CHAPTER 29

The lab report of the new evidence found in Vanderburgh's office came to Sgt. Flores's desk. It indicated that the residue was indeed from Amanita mushrooms. He felt he was getting somewhere; they had evidence of how Robert had ingested the stuff. Now the question was whether he had brewed his own coffee or someone else had done it for him. He called the crime lab and asked the technician who had been with him when the residue had been found whether he had fingerprinted the brewer and coffee can.

Yes, the technician had done so. He was running them through the national fingerprint database for a match. He didn't think there were good odds of finding a match. To be in the database, the prints would have been input from other agencies such as the military, police, and anyone who needed a security clearance. If there was a match, Flores would know who might have put the residue in the coffee brewer.

Surprisingly, there was a match. The fingerprint belonged to none other than Tom Davis. Flores had a suspect, an unbelievable one but a suspect nonetheless.

Flores went to talk to Davis despite his lieutenant's orders to stand down. What he hoped to prove was that Davis was not the culprit. He found Davis coming out of Clara Barton's office.

"Mr. Davis, is there somewhere we can go and talk?" Flores asked.

"Sure, but only if you call me Tom. Mr. Davis sounds so formal. Let's go to my office. We can talk without being disturbed."

"Mr. Davis, this is formal. I want to ask you a few questions about the death of Mr. Vanderburgh."

"All right, follow me."

They walked through the plant to Davis's office. Closing the door after Flores, Davis sat at his desk. "Please have a seat, Sergeant Flores. How can I help you?"

"First, Mr. Davis, I'd like to know how close you were to Vanderburgh. Did you ever go into his office when he wasn't there?"

"Sure I did. I'm the head of security. I went in on several occasions to check on things."

"What did you do exactly? Did you touch or move anything?"

"Of course. I moved things around to check to see if there were any bugs or anything suspicious. Hey! What's this all about?"

"We found your fingerprints in the office near the coffee brewer. We also found the substance that killed Vanderburgh near the brewer. I wonder how that could be. Did you ever brew coffee for Vanderburgh?"

"Yes, every morning. I went in to set the coffee up so it'd be fresh and hot when Rob came in. Am I a suspect? Do I need my attorney?"

"Only if you think you do. Everyone close to Vanderburgh is a suspect. I'm trying to find out the facts, and I'll be interviewing everyone. I started with you because of the fingerprints."

"You should have found others such as Clara's, Robert Junior's, Vivian's, and Madeline's."

"We did. As I said, I'll be talking to them."

"What else do you want to know?"

"What are you going to do now that you own part of the company? Will you be staying on as security chief?"

"As a matter of fact, Clara and I were discussing what my

role will be. We're still undecided. Why? Are you interested in the job?"

"Are you kidding? Only a fool wouldn't want to work here in any capacity. The problem is, I still have a couple of years before I can retire from the force. But we were talking about your plans and the future of the company as you see it. I need to know how Vanderburgh's death has benefitted you."

"Obviously, being part owner will benefit me greatly. My compensation package will be increasing along with other perks such as a company car, travel allowances, and an expense account. More than that, I'll have a say in the day-to-day operations. Clara wants me to be the VP of operations. Nice sounding, isn't it?"

"So you'll benefit a lot."

"I suppose so. What are you getting at? Do you think I had something to do with Rob's death? Why would I kill him? I didn't know what was in the will. How would I know I would become a part owner? I presumed that Robert Junior would inherit it all."

"I understand what you're saying. As I said, I'm trying to weed out the facts from fiction and supposition. I'm not accusing anybody yet."

"Okay, let's get to it. What do we do now?"

"I, not you, will interview each person involved and try to get some answers. I want you to stay out of it."

"I'm sure I could help in some way. I know the people more intimately than you do."

"You can help by staying out of it."

"Whatever you say, Sergeant," Davis said knowing full well that he was going to conduct his own investigation.

CHAPTER 30

People finally straggled out of the Vanderburghs' house. After Robert, Madeline, and her spouse left, Jason stayed back with Vivian, who dismissed the maids and caterers after they had cleaned up. Now they were finally alone.

"Jason, that was a nightmare. I'm exhausted. Thanks for staying. I don't think I could have done this without you."

"Viv, you're a strong woman. You're sure of yourself, and you could have made it without me or anybody else."

"I appreciate your saying those kind things."

She sat on the couch in the living room and patted the spot next to her. "Come here and sit with me. I need a shoulder to lean on."

Jason sat being careful not to be so close that they touched. He still wasn't sure how to react to Vivian's advances, but he was pleased that she found him attractive.

"How can I help, Viv? You should go to bed since you're so tired."

"Not right now. I need some comfort and compassion. Or maybe it's passionate loving that I need." She smiled at him.

"Viv, we should talk about what you're going to do with your life now that Robert's gone. Are you going to stay in this house or downsize?"

"Come on, Jason. I don't want to talk about that yet. I want to relax in your arms and think about nothing but us."

"But Viv, you just lost your husband and had the service for him and the funeral dinner. Should you be thinking about romance at this time?"

"Yes, Jason, I should. I told you that Robert and I hadn't lived as husband and wife for many years. I knew about Rob's and Clara's affair years ago. Why he didn't leave me for her I don't know. He loved her more than me if he ever did love me. Did you know he had a child with her? I hear she's a real beauty. She was at the funeral with her mother. I think her name's Veronica."

"No, I didn't know that. I was wondering who that pretty woman with Clara was. I imagine she may put a damper on the distribution of the company shares."

"How could she? Rob left nothing special to his family. She would have to fight the children for any of their shares. Besides, she'd have to prove she was Rob's daughter."

"That wouldn't be hard to do. It depends on how Clara listed the father. If she listed the father as Robert, that's all the proof needed. It wouldn't be hard to get a judge to agree that she deserved part."

"No! I won't let that happen. While I knew of Rob's liaison with Clara, I didn't condone it. I won't have an interloper come in and spoil it for my children. They've lost enough already."

"What do you plan on doing?"

"Right now, I'm going to relax as much as possible and not worry about it. I plan on following my urges. I plan on doing nothing but spending some more time with you. Now shut up and come cuddle me."

Jason knew it would be pointless to argue with her. He shifted on the couch, leaned her back into him, and put his arms around her slim waist. He stroked her hair and breathed in her fragrance. He felt he belonged there. Vivian sighed in Jason's arms.

CHAPTER 31

After the funeral dinner, Robert, still fuming about what his father had done to him, how Clara had talked to him, and finding out about another sister, went to his favorite watering hole. He needed space and time to plan his next move.

He ordered a Jack Daniel's and Coke. Sitting at a table in the back of the place, he scanned the room looking for anyone he knew. The dark room smelled like stale beer and liquor and faintly of cigarette smoke. A ban on smoking in public places had been in effect for years, but the owners of the bar had refused to do much cleaning to get rid of the smell.

He sipped his drink and relished the burn as it went down his throat. After he ordered another one, he spotted someone he hadn't seen in years, his father's attorney and confidant. Rob waved at him to come over. The man hesitated for a moment, but then suddenly recognizing Rob, he walked through the maze of tables.

"Hey Robert. I haven't seen you for a long time. How's it going? You still working for your father, or have you finally taken control?"

"No. The old man died the other day. We just had his memorial service today. He had the nerve to cut me out of my inheritance."

"What? What do you mean he died? What do you mean he cut you out? Did he change his will?"

"Clara found him at his desk slumped over and quite dead.

The police are investigating it as a homicide. It was probably a heart attack. He'd been working too much and was worried about Tamarac Electronics, his biggest competition. I believe he was trying to buy it to eliminate that threat."

"So what are you going to do now?"

"I'm going to contest the will. It was handwritten, and I don't believe it's genuine. Are you still a lawyer?"

"Yes I am, but I don't practice much anymore. Why do you ask?"

"Can I trust you to keep something confidential?"

"Sure. I still have client-attorney privileges. There is still a confidentiality clause. How can I help?"

"I told you that I want to contest the will. I don't have the money to do it. I've contacted Tamara Hayes, Tamarac's owner, about helping me out. She said she would front all the money I needed but that she wanted a hundred percent of the company. I told her that that was too much."

"So you want me to handle the contest free of charge or at a reduced rate."

"Yes, I suppose that's what I'm asking. Will you do it? How much would it cost?"

"I'll do it on one condition."

"What's that?"

"You will under no circumstances sell the company or any part of it to Tamara Hayes. If you did, your father would have a fit."

"I had no plans to sell it if I gain controlling interest in it. I also want to get rid of Clara Barton and her daughter. I want to run the company myself."

"Okay, call my office tomorrow and make an appointment so we can talk about what I'll need to proceed. Bring a copy of the present will and any previous ones you have. Are we going to include the rest of the family in the contestation? If so, I'll need their signed and notarized permissions. If not, they have to be present too."

"I wasn't planning on including the family. What do you think? Would it be better if I did?"

"Yes, it would be. Get their information and whether they want to proceed. Try to bring them with you so they'll understand all this will entail. See you soon."

CHAPTER 32

The next day, Robert called the attorney; he wanted to contest the legality of the will and thus stop Clara and Tom from inheriting the company. The complaint had to go to the probate court for a decision. The attorney immediately filed the paperwork asking for a quick decision. The probate judge took the complaint under immediate consideration and that stopped the proceedings to distribute the wealth right away.

When the judge read the complaint, however, she laughed. She couldn't believe Robert was naive enough to think he could reverse the will. She quickly dismissed the case as frivolous and pointless. The will had been signed, witnessed, and filed in the courts; it was valid.

Robert couldn't believe it. His lawyer had told him that it was sure to be reversed. He was desperate to get control of his father's company. *I can still talk to Tamara. She was willing to listen to my proposal at least. But she demanded too much in return for the money she would have invested.* She had wanted full control of the company, and he would still be out on the street. He could not let Vanderburgh Electronics out of the family's and most especially his control.

He left the courtroom disgruntled, but he was determined to fight for what he believed was rightfully his. He didn't know what to do or how to go about doing it. He thought about asking

Tamara if she had any ideas. He didn't want anyone in the family to know what he was planning.

He called Tamara.

"Hello, Robert. To what do I owe this pleasure? How can I help you?"

"Hi, Tammy. You know I want to gain control of Dad's company. I was wondering if you had any ideas about how and what to do."

"Well, Rob, that's some favor. You're the one who turned my proposal down, and now you want my help? I don't see the profit in it for me."

"Yes I know. But you started your own business from scratch, and look where you are now. I need some advice, but I don't want the family to know what I'm doing, so I can't ask any of them or the lawyers."

"Again, how would I benefit from helping you? Vanderburgh is my biggest competition."

"I know I'm asking a lot of you. But maybe at some point down the road, we could merge our companies and make us the biggest electronics firm in the state, maybe even the nation. How does that sound? I don't like the idea of Dad's company run by a floozy of a secretary."

"Let me think about it for a couple of days. I'll see what I can come up with."

"Okay, but make it quick. I'm anxious to get this done so that Clara doesn't get used to being in charge."

"Goodbye, Rob," Tamara said sweetly as she hung up and started thinking about how she could get Robert to give her the company.

That evening, Robert went to celebrate this minor victory at his favorite bar.

CHAPTER 33

Jason was still trying to comfort Vivian. She was inconsolable after what Robert had said at the funeral.

"Come on, Viv, you need to lighten up a bit. You knew what your husband had been doing with his secretary. Surely you knew how it would affect Rob when he found out. I don't find his outrage particularly upsetting."

"Of course you wouldn't! You're not his mother. If he had anything to say, he should have talked to me first. I could have settled him down."

"Maybe, but he has some anger issues about being cut out of the will and thinking his father's mistress would get control of the company he was expecting to inherit. Why don't you come over here and let me hold you?"

"That's exactly what I want," she said as she slipped into his waiting arms.

CHAPTER 34

Robert woke up with a splitting headache. Not remembering much about what happened the previous night except his conversation with Tamara, he turned the TV on only to find Tamara's picture displayed behind the commentator's face. The commentator was saying something about Tamara, but Rob hadn't been able to focus yet. Then he noticed the scrolling banner at the bottom of the screen: "Tamara Hayes found dead!"

What? Rob thought. *There must be some mistake. I spoke with her just last night.*

The commentator said, "Miss Hayes was found this morning by her secretary when she came into work. It is unknown at this time whether foul play was involved, but based on some comments by police officers, it's a good possibility. Police say they're looking for a person of interest at this time. It is known that Robert Vanderburgh Junior was in conversation with Miss Hayes about merging the two companies. He is thought to be distraught over his father's changing his will just before his untimely death. Some speculate that the negotiations with Miss Hayes did not go very well prompting police to want to talk to Mr. Vanderburgh. More from reporters on the scene later."

Rob couldn't believe it. He was a suspect. For sure, he didn't remember the night very well, but he was sure that he hadn't seen Tamara after speaking with her on the phone. He thought about contacting Rory and Madeline and asking for their advice. That was funny—asking his drunken brother and his airhead sister for advice. Maybe he should contact his mom he thought.

He sat on the couch and buried his face in his hands. "What should I do?" he asked aloud.

The commentator was continuing. "The police are saying now that Miss Hayes's death could have been racially motivated. Miss Hayes was a bright graduate of Lawrence Tech who had built her company from scratch to one of the largest electronics in the state. She was also black. Robert Vanderburgh Junior is white. And in other news …"

Rob couldn't believe it. He liked Tamara, but as her competitor, he had some fierce discussions about where to take the two companies even though Vanderburgh Electronics wasn't legally his. He still was plotting how to get control of the company his father had built.

CHAPTER 35

Sergeant Flores, at that point saddled with two homicides, wondered if they were related. He mentally slugged through what facts he had. Robert Sr. had died of poisoning from a mushroom. He had not ingested the poison purposely. There was mushroom dust by the coffee maker in his office. Tamara Hayes had died suddenly and mysteriously. Autopsy results were not yet in.

Next, he listed the people who would benefit from each of the deaths: Robert Jr., supposed heir; Clara Barton, secretary and named heir; Tom Davis, head of security; Tamara by acquisition; Vivian; and Madeline.

Flores rolled his eyes at the possibilities. He immediately crossed Vivian's name off the list; he couldn't see her killing her meal ticket. Neither could he picture Madeline cutting off the supply of money and her house. That left Robert, Clara Barton, Tom Davis, and Tamara. Each had a motive, but did each have the opportunity? No, Tamara wouldn't have been able to get that close in Robert's office. He crossed her off the list too for the time being. But Robert, Clara Barton, and Tom Davis had plenty of opportunities to access Robert Sr.'s office, and they all had motives.

He thought about eliminating Robert because he didn't inherit enough of the company to have control over it. But then, he didn't know that his father had changed the will to exclude him from the rest of the stock thereby not gaining controlling interest in the company.

What did Clara and Tom gain? Controlling interest in the company. What did they know about the change in the will? Could they have conspired to kill Robert to get the company?

Based on the final list, Flores decided to make some inquiries into the finances of the three remaining suspects. His first choice was Robert. Pulling Rob's driver's license, credit report, and banking information, he found that while Rob had a substantial amount of debt, he was not in dire need of money. Flores thought he might be power hungry, which could be a motive, but it looked to Flores that he could be put on the bottom of the list for the time being.

Clara's reports were similar to Rob's. She seemed solvent, but she had a disabled daughter who needed constant care. It cost her about $3,500 a month to keep Sam in a nursing home.

Tom's information was very interesting. He had much more debt than others with the same income; it appeared that he needed money quickly. Did he have prior knowledge of the will change? How was he racking up that much debt? Some thoughts started to gel in Flores's mind. Davis owed a lot of money. He had access to Vanderburgh's office. He had opportunities to enter the office and brew coffee before Vanderburgh arrived for the day. Flores wondered how likely it would be for Davis to poison his boss, a good friend.

Flores called Vanderburgh Electronics to see if Davis was available. Much to his surprise, Davis was not in and hadn't been for several days. No one knew where he was. Flores called Davis at his home, but the call went straight to a full voice mailbox. Red flags went up immediately. Flores drove to Davis's house. His car was in the driveway, and mail was stuffed in his mailbox. Flores walked up to the porch and peered through the open curtains. He saw nothing, so he rang the bell. No one answered. He rang again. No answer. He went around to the back of the house. The patio door was closed. The drapes were closed. Flores returned to his squad car and called for backup. He had reason to believe something was wrong. While he waited for backup, he searched the yard for any clues.

Flores found evidence of a big dog, but there had been no barking when he rang the bell. That made him wonder where the dog was.

When backup arrived, Flores broke the kitchen door windows with the butt of his handgun. He reached in, unlocked the door, and opened it. He entered cautiously with gun still in hand. Nothing in the kitchen or the living room. Flores continued throughout the rest of the house. There was nothing unusual. No signs of foul play. No signs of anything. No dog. No human being. Nothing. Flores was puzzled by the absence of any indication that anyone lived there. The rest of the backup searched the basement and also found nothing.

Flores decided to call in the forensics team. He instructed them to search everything as if the house were a crime scene. The forensic team went at it professionally leaving nothing alone. They dusted for fingerprints. They checked trash cans and the books on the bookshelves to see if there was a hidden safe. They found nothing unusual as did the detectives. Another mystery was not what Flores needed. He closed up the house and put crime tape around the front porch and the patio. Then he drove back to his office.

He went over all the things he knew about the two murders and the missing Tom Davis, which wasn't much. Vanderburgh had been poisoned in his office while drinking coffee. He had changed his will to exclude the children and especially Robert. He had named his longtime secretary principal recipient along with Tom Davis being named secondary. The children still had their seven percent each. None of the children knew that Senior had changed his will. Autopsy results for Tamara Hayes were not in yet. Davis was missing.

As Flores was pondering these facts, a detective appeared at his door with an interoffice memo envelope. "Sir," she said, "This report from the coroner came a few minutes ago."

"Please put it on my desk."

Flores stared at the envelope for a moment before he picked it up. He wanted to know what the results were, but he was hesitant. He had a hunch about what the report would say about the cause of Tamara's death. Flores opened the envelope and started reading the report. As he had expected, Tamara had been poisoned by Amanita mushrooms. Robert had the opportunities and motives for the deaths of his father and Tamara. Robert also wanted Tom Davis out of the way. Who was next? Clara? With Clara and Tom out of the way, Junior could have the will declared null, and he would be the owner of Vanderburgh Electronics. With Tamara gone, he could buy her company to eliminate the competition.

Flores sent a detective to obtain an arrest warrant for Robert and search warrants for his office and home. When the warrants were issued, Flores sent one of his detectives to arrest Robert and several others to search his home while he went to Vanderburgh's office.

Robert was in his office; the detective sent to arrest him read him his Miranda rights. He started to help Flores search the office. They looked in the desk drawers, file cabinets, and Robert's washroom. In the toilet tank, they found a plastic bag full of mushrooms. The detectives left the office with Robert, whom they put in the back seat of a squad car.

Flores left Robert sit in an interrogation room at the police station to think about what he had done. Flores was pretty sure that he would ask for his lawyer, but the sergeant wanted to let him stew for a while.

When Flores entered the interrogation room, Rob had his head on the table and was sitting calmly. Flores sat on the opposite side of the table, placed a cup of coffee on it, and cleared his throat.

Rob looked up, showing no concern a tall. He thought he had been unfairly arrested.

Flores started in. "Where were you the night your father died?"

"I was in my office until about nine. Then I went home to be with my wife."

"Can she vouch for you?"

"Probably not. She was in bed when I got home, and I worked some more in my office at home."

"Well, that could be a problem for you. Did anyone see you in either office?"

"No. But I called Tamara from home."

"She's dead. What did you talk to her about?"

"About financing my try to break my dad's will. She was not receptive to my proposal. She did tell me she would help me if I would then turn the company over to her. What would be the point? What do you think I did? Kill my dad and Tamara?"

"That's exactly what I think. Did you?"

"No. That's nuts. I loved my dad, and I wanted to do business with Tamara. Why would I kill either of them?"

"How do you explain the mushrooms in your office?"

"I don't know how they got there. I certainly didn't put them there. Have you checked with Tom Davis?"

"He's missing. What would his motive be?"

"He wanted my father's company almost as much as I did. I think he coerced my dad into changing his will. I think he had Dad include him in the will cutting me out."

"You think so? What do you base that on? Did Davis say anything to you to indicate what he wanted?"

"No. It's just a feeling I have."

"We're talking about you right now. You had the motive, the opportunity, and the means to kill Tamara and your dad. Where did you get the mushrooms?"

"I already told you that I don't know where they came from.

I didn't know that the bag was in the commode. I suggest you concentrate on finding Davis."

"I don't have any reason to suspect Davis of anything other than being out of town, so I'll continue to hold you. This time, I'm going to put you in a cell. Maybe you'll think about how serious this is."

Flores left the interrogation room and told a detective to lock Rob up. He called Connor, a detective, into his office. "Find Tom Davis. I heard he has a cabin up north somewhere. He might be there. Also, pull a search warrant for Davis's home and office."

"Okay, boss. Do you want me to conduct the searches?"

"You do the one of Davis's office. Tell Schmidt to do the house. Maybe Schmidt should take the CSI unit again."

CHAPTER 36

Tom Davis decided to take a vacation to his cabin near Petoskey, Michigan. He was also hiding out, waiting for Robert to be formally indicted for the murders of Tamara and Robert Sr. Davis felt he was safe. He was sure that there was no evidence against him. No one knew that he had Robert change his will just before he died.

It had been a stroke of genius. He had Robert make Clara Barton principal owner and him secondary excluding his sons and daughter. He knew that without Robert Senior and Junior in the way, he was going to control the company because Clara would follow his lead and advice. He planted the bag of mushrooms in Rob's office to frame him. He hoped that Rob would be blamed for Tamara's death.

Davis didn't think anyone knew about his hideaway. The property was in his wife's maiden name. Little did he know of Conner's tenacity.

Detective Conner first checked for a marriage license. He found that Davis was indeed married. Then he looked for properties listed in both Davis's and his wife's names. He found a property near Petoskey that was registered in Davis's wife's name.

Conner called Flores with what he had found. He wanted to know if he should get search and arrest warrants there or call the Petoskey PD to handle that. Flores asked how far Petoskey was from them; Conner said approximately 265 miles. Flores told

Conner to get the warrants and call the Petoskey PD to let them know he was on his way. They might be able to watch Davis's place and assist Conner on the takedown and search of the cabin.

Conner left to obtain the warrants and then start the drive north. He called the Petoskey PD on his way; they let him know that they were well acquainted with Davis and would watch his place.

CHAPTER 37

J ason called Vivian.

"Hello?" Vivian answered.

"Hello, Viv. I was wondering if you'd like to go out to dinner with me."

"Oh hi, Jason. How are you doing?"

"I'm doing fine. I've been missing you, however. I wanted to hear your voice and see you again."

"My, aren't you sweet? What did you have in mind?"

"I thought we could go to dinner and maybe catch a movie … Then who knows?"

"That sounds delightful. I've missed you too. All this death and turmoil that they've caused is too much for me to handle on my own. I need someone to lean on."

"That's great! How 'bout I pick you up at seven?"

"That sounds fine. What should I wear?"

"Anything would be fine. Casual would probably be best."

"Okay, see you then. Bye for now, Jason."

CHAPTER 38

When Detective Connor arrived at the Petoskey police department, he was pleasantly surprised to find out that Davis had turned himself in. Conner still had to search the cabin for any evidence. Much to his surprise, he found Clara Barton and her daughter, Veronica, there. He asked them to step outside and wait on the porch while he searched the cabin. He didn't expect to find much because it was evident that they had been forewarned about his coming.

Conner looking in all the kitchen cabinets and the dishwasher. The refrigerator and the stove were next. As he suspected, he found nothing. Moving on, he searched the living room and then the small bedroom and bathroom.

His next stop was the master suite, where he found a staircase leading to the attic. Cautiously, he searched through the bedroom, focusing on the closet, the dresser drawers, and under the bed. He still found nothing, so he went to the master bathroom and searched the trash and the medicine cabinet. He removed the toilet tank lid and found a baggie full of mushroom dust. Replacing the lid, he proceeded to the attic, where he found a lot of electronic equipment still in their packaging from Vanderburgh Electronics. There were some things from Tamarac Electronics as well.

The more he discovered, the more confusing things became. He guessed that Davis was stockpiling this equipment in the event that he would gain control of Vanderburgh's company, but why Davis had Tamarac's electronics was a mystery.

Conner collected the evidence he found and asked Clara and Veronica to accompany him back to the police station in his car. He put the evidence in the trunk and the women in the back seat. He had not arrested them yet. They were not handcuffed, but the doors wouldn't open from the inside.

The trip to the station took only a few minutes. Conner opened the rear door and helped the women out. He escorted them into the station, where he was greeted by a lieutenant whose name tag read Harrison. He asked Conner what the women were doing there.

"Lieutenant, these women are material witnesses. I brought them in from Davis's cabin. I need to ask them a few questions about two murders I'm working on in Wayne County. Is there an interview room I can put them in? Would you also put Davis in a separate room?"

"Will do. Do you need some assistance questioning them?"

"No, I don't think so, but maybe have a guard stationed outside Davis's room."

"I'll put Davis in room one and the women in room three. Call me if you need anything."

"No problem. Thanks, Lieutenant."

Detective Conner entered room one and sauntered to the table, where Davis was seated in one of the two chairs. Conner sat across from Davis and was silent for several minutes trying to get Davis to sweat a bit before he said, "Hi, Tom. How are you? Mind if I ask you a few questions?"

"Sure, Detective. I don't mind. I could use a bottle of water or some coffee."

"Maybe later. Why were you up here with Clara and her daughter?"

"Since Clara and I are now the majority owners of Vanderburgh, we thought it was prudent to plan for how we wanted the company to grow and expand. Veronica, Clara's daughter, is a CPA and architect. We thought she could help us make sense of the company's books. Robert Senior had his own method for keeping the books, and he did all the accounting himself. He didn't want anyone else to know how profitable the company was. We thought it would be best to get out of town so we wouldn't be disturbed. The cabin was a convenient place."

"How do you explain the lack of guns at the cabin? It is a hunting cabin, isn't it?"

"I bring my guns up here only when I'm going hunting."

"Why were there no guns at your house?"

"My wife doesn't like guns at all. She insists I not keep them at the house."

"Where do you keep them? How do you get them when you want them?"

"My sons keep them at their houses. They bring them to me when I need them."

"Okay, that makes sense. How do you explain the mushroom dust we found in your toilet?"

"Wait! What? I don't understand. I didn't put that there."

"Yeah. I hear that a lot. Now's the time to come clean and tell me what you did."

"I did nothing! I had nothing to do with that mushroom dust. Wait. Am I a suspect? Should I have a lawyer?"

Conner looked at Davis as he got up and walked to the door. He did not answer Davis's questions. In the corridor, Conner leaned against the door to the interview room. He breathed a big sigh of frustration. He knew that it was unlikely he would get a confession.

He entered room three. Clara and Veronica were seated in two chairs on one side of the table; Connor sat in a chair across from them. He smiled and asked, "Ladies, are you comfortable? Is there anything I can get you?"

"No," Clara said. "You can tell us why you have us here and what you want."

"Let's see. You were with one of the prime suspects in the murders of Vanderburgh and Hayes. That makes you either accomplices or material witnesses. Which is it?"

"You can't be serious. Are you accusing us of aiding and abetting? Did Tom have anything to do with those deaths?"

"That's what I'm trying to find out. I'm not accusing anybody of anything yet. Would you tell me why you're up here with Tom?"

"Since he and I are majority stockholders, he thought it would be best to discuss what we wanted to do with the company, you know, how to make it grow and continue to prosper. My daughter is a CPA and an architect, and Tom thought she would be able to make sense of the books. You might not know, but Robert kept the books himself."

"Do you know how Vanderburgh and Hayes were killed?"

"Weren't they poisoned?" asked Clara.

"Yes, that's right. Are you familiar with Amanita mushrooms?"

Veronica said, "I think they can be deadly in sufficient quantity. Why are you asking?"

"I found a large quantity in the toilet in the cabin. It's what caused Vanderburgh's and Hayes's deaths. Do you know anything about that?"

"Of course not!" Clara exclaimed. "Just what are you implying?"

"I'm not implying anything, Mrs. Barton. I'm trying to find out the truth. Just to be clear, you know nothing of how the mushroom dust found its way into the toilet tank?"

"I already told you no. Don't you listen? My daughter doesn't either."

"I hear very well. I'm making sure there was no mistake. Why don't you let Veronica speak for herself? Veronica, do you know anything about the dust?"

"I saw Tom take a large baggie into the bathroom right after we got here. He didn't come out with it."

"That certainly changes things. Do you know what motive Tom would have for killing Vanderburgh and Hayes?"

"I think that's obvious," Clara said. "Tom wanted to gain control of the company. He may have coerced Robert to change his will. He may have thought that Robert changed it in favor of him. I don't know about Tamara. Why would he have killed her? It's possible that he thought he could have gotten control of her company. Has her will been read yet?"

"That's an interesting speculation. What makes you think that's possible?"

"I know Tom met with Tamara several times right before she died. I thought she was trying to buy Vanderburgh. I know she wanted it badly."

"Do you know anything about Tom's debt? Could he be struggling to make ends meet?"

"I doubt it. I guess it's possible that he has a drug problem or gambling. He was paid good money by Robert. Also, his wife is a professor at the University of Michigan. I think she works at the Dearborn campus."

"That helps quite a bit. Do you know what department she's in? Do you know how the Davis's relationship is?"

"No, Detective, I don't know about their relationship. I believe she's in the computer science or electrical engineering department."

"Hmm. That's interesting. Can you think of anything else that might help even if you think it's trivial?"

"No," Clara said.

"If you happen to remember anything, let me know. Sit tight for a few minutes longer while I go ask Tom a few more questions."

Conner left the room.

CHAPTER 39

Harold Pfeiffer, Tamara Hayes's attorney, called Flores. "Sergeant Flores, I'm trying to get in touch with the principals named in Ms. Hayes's will. I can't find them. Do you know where they might be?"

"Hey Harold. I don't know if I can help you. I don't know their names."

"I'm looking for Tom Davis and Clara Barton. Do you happen to know where they are?"

"Tom and Clara? Interesting. They're in the Petoskey PD being questioned."

"Can I get hold of them? I need to process the will. They're both named to inherit Tamarac Electronics."

"No, they're in custody. Can you tell me the gist of the will?"

"Sure. I don't suppose it would hurt anything. Tom is given the majority of the stock, and Clara has the remainder."

"When was the will written?"

"Tamara came in the day before she died. She looked reluctant to change it, almost as if she was being forced to change it."

"I'll contact my detective in Petoskey and let him know of these developments. Thank you for calling me."

Flores called the Petoskey PD and asked to speak with Detective Connor. The desk sergeant told him that Conner was interviewing Davis. "Will you please have him call me right away?" Flores asked.

"Sure thing, Sergeant. Is it important enough to interrupt him?"

"Yes it is. I'll wait."

After listening to some elevator music, Flores heard the click of a receiver being picked up.

"Detective Conner here. How can I help you?"

"Conner, this is Flores. Don't release Davis under any circumstances. I have information that could provide a motive for Tamara Hayes's death. It looks like she was coerced into changing her will. Guess who the main beneficiary is? None other than Tom Davis, and Clara Barton was named secondary.

I found a stash of mushroom dust in the toilet and lots of stolen electronic equipment in the attic."

"I'll use the arrest warrant I have to arrest Davis. I'll bring him back first thing in the morning. What do you want me to do with Mrs. Barton and her daughter?"

"If you have room in your car, bring them in too. If not, see if Petoskey will keep them until I can get another car up there. They may be accomplices or material witnesses."

"I think I can get them all in my car."

"Recheck the cabin for anything you may have missed. Pay particular attention to any jewelry boxes. Search for hidden doors. Tear the place apart if you have to."

"Okay, Sergeant. Do you want me to let you know if I find anything?"

"Yes, and I don't care about the time of day."

Conner had new marching orders. He went to find the Petoskey lieutenant who had helped him. "Lieutenant, I'm arresting Tom Davis for the murders. Could you hold him until tomorrow morning? Also, can you give the ladies better accommodations than a cell? I need to take them back with me."

"I think I can come up with something."

"Thanks, Lieutenant. I appreciate it."

Conner left for the cabin hoping to get the second search done quickly. He entered the cabin and went directly to the master bedroom. He did a cursory look at all the surfaces before looking in the closet for any hidden compartments. Finding a small door that he had missed earlier, he cautiously opened it to reveal a wall safe. He would have to wait for a locksmith to come to open it up or trash it as Flores had told him to do if necessary.

He found a pry bar in the garage and headed back to the closet. He put the pry bar beneath the lip of the dial lock and started to apply pressure. The lock was strong, but he heard straining and groaning. It suddenly snapped. Inside the safe, Conner found a huge bag of uncut mushrooms, a stack of hundred-dollar bills, and a Glock 17, more than enough to convict Davis. But of what? Did this prove beyond a shadow of a doubt that he had poisoned Vanderburgh and Hayes? Conner doubted it, so he kept looking.

He went to the dresser and concentrated on the drawers; the bottom one had a false bottom. He slid the panel aside and saw what looked like reports and other papers about Vanderburgh Electronics and Tamarac Electronics. Conner thought he had enough, but he continued to search. He entered the kitchen and looked through the refrigerator and the freezer and found nothing. He looked in the cupboards, taking the coffee can out and emptying the grounds. Eureka. He found the mother lode. In the coffee can were documents that talked about Davis's desire to take over both companies, plans to intimidate Vanderburgh and Hayes to change their wills, and plans to kill them.

Conner stayed in a motel that night and headed back to the police department in the morning. He cuffed Davis and put him in the back seat with Clara while Veronica rode up front with him. The drive back to Livonia was uneventful.

After booking Davis, Conner went to see Flores. Conner wanted to take the rest of the afternoon off and be able to get started again fresh in the morning.

Flores said, "Sure. Get some rest. You deserve it. You can hit it first thing in the morning."

Conner went home and immediately jumped into the shower. He shaved and put on some comfy clothes. He went to his bedroom, lay down, and was asleep in a matter of a few minutes.

CHAPTER 40

T he next morning was gloomy and overcast with thunderstorms approaching from the west. It didn't look like it was going to be a pleasant day.

Conner drove to the police station, which was on the southeast corner of Farmington and Five Mile Roads and surrounded by grassy areas, the courthouse, and the library. It was an ideal place that afforded easy access to the three areas most visited by lawyers and citizens alike.

There was an ambulance with lights flashing parked by the side entrance where police officers entered. As he got to the door, the attendants were wheeling their stretcher out. On it lay Tom Davis. Conner stopped the attendants. "Wait! that's my prisoner. Where are you taking him, and why was I not told?"

"Sir, it appears he tried to commit suicide. Luckily, one of the guards was able to stanch the flow of blood from his arms or he might be going to the morgue instead of the hospital."

"Which hospital are you taking him to?"

"Saint Mary's just down the street."

"I'll be down there soon."

Conner went to the squad room, sat at his desk, and put his head in his hands muttering to himself. Gathering himself, Conner went to see Flores.

"Sergeant, why wasn't I told about Davis's problem? I need to continue to interview him about the murders. He hasn't lawyered up, has he?"

"No, Conner, he hasn't. He tried to take the coward's way out. He'll be okay in a few days. You can continue with him then."

"What would you like me to do it the interim?"

"Catch up on your paperwork, but I know you'd rather be doing something exciting. Why don't you return to Davis's house and see if you can find any more evidence?"

"Sounds good. I think I'll talk to the ladies some more too."

Conner left the station but proceeded to the hospital; he wanted to see how critical Davis was. He entered the ER and looked for the head nurse. She was bending over her computer with a frown. "Hey Susan! How ya doing? I haven't seen you in a while. What's your patient load?"

"Hi, Sean. I'm doing fine, but it's a nuthouse in here with suicide attempts, drug overdoses, babies wanting to come early, heart attacks ... You know, the normal things in an ER."

"Yeah I know. Speaking of suicide attempts, how's Tom Davis doing?"

"Who? I never heard of him. When did he come in?"

"Wait. What? He was a prisoner brought in from the police station. He was my prisoner. Supposedly, he tried to commit suicide in his cell. The ambulance attendants said they were bringing him here. Where else might they have taken him?"

"I don't know. Maybe Botsford or even Garden City."

"Why would they change where they were taking him?"

"We may have been so busy that we had to send them to a different hospital."

Conner called Flores to report the missing prisoner. When Flores heard that Conner had disobeyed his orders, he was furious and read Conner the riot act. "I told you to leave it alone for now. Why did you go to the hospital anyway? I told you to investigate further in Davis's house and talk to the women. I specifically told you to not go to the hospital. I ought to suspend you or put you on desk duty for insubordination.

"Conner, you're a good detective and someday will make a fine sergeant. You think on your feet, you show initiative, but you gotta get it through your thick head that you must obey orders. Instead, I'm going to allow you to pursue Davis's disappearance."

"Thanks, Sergeant. You won't regret your decision. I promise that if I get any bright ideas, I'll run them by you before acting on them."

Conner left the hospital; he had a hunch about where Davis might be.

CHAPTER 41

Vivian was going stir-crazy sitting in the big house by herself, so she called Jason. She guessed he was probably busy at work, but she had to hear his voice.

"Harold Pfeiffer and associates. This is Sheila. How may I help you?"

"Hi, Sheila, this is Mrs. Vanderburgh. Is Jason in?"

"Yes ma'am. May I tell him which Mrs. Vanderburgh?"

"Oh. Yes. This is Vivian Vanderburgh."

"One moment please."

Vivian waited impatiently; she hated elevator music.

"Hello, this is Jason. How can I be of assistance to you?"

"Hi, Jason," Vivian said breathlessly. "I'll tell you how you can assist me. You can come over right now and cuddle with me. I need some loving time."

"Ah, Viv, I'm with a client. Can I call you back in half an hour?"

"Yeah," she said pouting. "I guess that would be all right."

Viv hung up. Looking around her bedroom, she decided that it could use a good cleaning and new furniture. She called her maid. "Alice, I want you to clean this room so that it can pass a white-glove inspection. And get some bedroom furniture salesmen to come here with some samples. I want everything gone out of here."

"Yes ma'am. Do you want the salespeople to bring in actual samples or will pictures be enough?"

"Pictures, silly. Tell them that I intend to buy a whole new ensemble. Oh, and tell them I'll need it delivered and set up today."

Vivian went down to the kitchen to see if there were any sweet morsels around. Just as she arrived in the kitchen, her phone rang. "Hello?"

"Hi, Viv. It's Jason. What's wrong? What can I do for you?"

"You can come here and make love with me. But I suppose that's not possible right now."

"No, Viv, it's not possible right now. I have another client coming in a few minutes. I can be over there right after work if that's okay."

"Well, okay, if your client is more important than I am to you," she whined.

"He's not more important than you, but I can't be jumping over there every time a flea passes gas."

"Yes I know, Jason, but I miss you so much. Try to be here for dinner around sevenish. I'll have Cookie make one of her delightful surprises. No, you won't have to bring the wine."

"I'm well aware that you're a very rich woman and a very desirable and attractive one at that. You don't have to buy my affection. I'm in your corner already."

"Corner? I would like you to be somewhere else than in a corner."

"Vivian! Let me get back to work."

"Oh, all right. See you at seven. Don't be late—snicker, snicker."

CHAPTER 42

Robert sat at his desk pondering what he was going to do next at the company his father had established and built up since his father had left it to that floozy Clara Barton and that backstabber Tom Davis. Rob was still dumbfounded that his dad had cut him out of the will almost completely.

He called Davis's office only to be informed that he had left for the weekend. His secretary wouldn't tell Rob where he went, or maybe she just didn't know.

Rob called to the front office for Clara. He was told that she was out for the remainder of the weekend and would be back Monday morning. He would have to wait until Monday to talk to either of them.

He called accounting. "Can I get copies of the past three years' P&L statements, please, as soon as possible?"

"No sir, that's not possible."

"What? Why not? I'm the VP of operations. I need them for planning the future of this company including your job."

"Sir, Mrs. Barton told me no one was to get any information until further notice. She said you are no longer VP of anything. Tom Davis concurs."

"When did this all come down?"

"Right before Mrs. Barton left for the weekend."

Well, Rob thought, *maybe I should just go home and wait.*

Across town, at the Do Drop Inn, Rory was systematically squandering his inheritance on booze and women. "Hey Johnny, bring me another one and a round for the guys. Remember, I'm not drinking well whiskey now. I'll have a double Chivas Regal. Oh yeah, and leave the bottle."

Rory somehow got it through his drunken stupor that he was now a multimillionaire. His father had died and left him seven percent of Vanderburgh Electronics. He had set it up so that Rory, Robert, and Madeline would receive their inheritance as a trust, meaning they would each get a monthly stipend. That was fine with Rory because he had never had so much money at his disposal. The amount he received was approximately $10,000 a month.

Madeline decided that stewing about her inheritance would be nonproductive, so she went to the gym to see her personal trainer. Of course they didn't do much training. Then she went to the beauty parlor to get her hair done and then to the nail salon, things she would have done anyway.

CHAPTER 43

Conner drove to Barton's house, where he found Clara and Veronica in the kitchen eating a late breakfast of scrambled eggs, sausage, English muffins, and coffee. It smelled really good, and Conner remembered he hadn't eaten anything yet.

Clara asked the detective to sit with them. "Please, Detective Conner, eat with us or at least have a cup of good Kona coffee."

"Yes, please do," Veronica added. "We have plenty, and you're more than welcome," she said batting her eyes at the handsome detective.

"No thanks on the breakfast, but I'll have some coffee. I have to ask you a few more questions I'm afraid."

Veronica got up to pour a steaming cup of coffee for the detective and brought it back to him. "Here you go, Detective. Cream or sugar?" She looked directly into his eyes while she sat a little closer to him.

"No thanks, miss. I prefer mine hot, black, and strong."

"Coffee or women?" she asked.

"Yes ma'am," he said not thinking about the question and her obvious flirting. "Tom tried to commit suicide at the jailhouse last night. He was being transported to the hospital to get checked out when he went missing. The hospital had no idea where he was because he never arrived. Do you have any ideas where he might be?"

"No. The only places I know he has are his house here and the cabin in Petoskey. You might try his sons' houses. I know they're close," Clara said.

"Good idea. I will. Thanks. Now what is your relationship with Davis?"

"It's rather complicated. Tom's my brother. When Robert hired him as the head of security, I became sort of his boss. So with the will giving us the majority of the company, I'm his boss outright. We've agreed to operate the company together. I own the majority of the shares, but I have decided it's in both of our interests to be united in our efforts. He'll continue as the head of security until he can find a suitable replacement. He'll also be the VP of operations."

"So, what I see is that both of you benefitted from Robert's death. Did you know anything about the change of the will?"

"Why of course not. I would have protested and made him change it back. I thought Rob would do fine at the helm."

Veronica chimed in. "I didn't know either. I didn't know that Mr. Vanderburgh was my father. As you can imagine, that came as quite a shock."

"Yes, I can imagine."

"I might add that I did not benefit except through my mother."

"How is it then that you're to become the head of accounting?"

"That too is complicated. The present CFO is about to retire. He was more or less a figurehead for the feds. He didn't do much because Mr. Vanderburgh kept the books himself. He made a mess of things from what I've seen so far. It will be up to me to fix them up and make sure that everything is aboveboard."

Conner said, "As I see it, you did benefit because now you have a cushy job working with your mother and uncle."

"Yes, I can see how you can think that. Detective Conner, are you married?" Veronica asked.

"No ma'am. What does have to do with the investigation?"

"Not much," Veronica said. "I was just wondering."

"Okay, let's get back to it. Does either of you know which son Davis is closer to?"

Clara answered, "I don't know, but it would seem to me Tom was closer to his elder son."

"Good. Do you know where he lives?"

"Somewhere here in Livonia," Clara said.

"Yeah. He's south of Ann Arbor Trail near Hines Drive. I think his house backs up onto the park," Veronica added.

"Okay, thanks, ladies. You've been a great help. Please don't go out of town without first notifying me of your intentions. And thanks for the coffee. It was very good."

Clara and Veronica walked Conner to the door and waited until he had driven away before breathing easier.

"Wow! That was close," Clara said.

"Wow! That was some man!" Veronica exclaimed. "Wait! What do you mean that was close?"

"I'm just glad Conner didn't ask to see the rest of the house. He might have found some evidence of Tom's having been here."

"You mean Uncle Tom was here?"

"No, dear. I mean he is here. I helped him get away from the hospital."

"Why on earth would you do that?"

"Because he's my brother, and I know he coerced old man Vanderburgh into changing the will. He was trying to look out for you, your sister, and me."

"I thought you liked the old man. He was my father after all."

"Yeah, I loved Rob, but he wouldn't dump his wife and marry me. He said it would cost him a fortune. He did take care of your sister's health needs, but I knew I wasn't in his will."

"This is unbelievable," Ronnie stated.

"You better believe it, sweetheart," said Ronnie's uncle as he appeared as if out of nowhere.

"Uncle Tom, you startled me! Where were you? Where do you come from? How did you get here?"

"Like the good detective said, I faked a suicide. Your mom had bribed the ambulance attendants to bring me here. When the two of you got here, I hid in the basement. There's a hidden room with a door that's almost impossible to see."

"I think I deserve an explanation or two."

"So right you are, sweet pea. When I found out that your mom was not going to get a thing after all that Rob had put her through, I knew something had to change. One day, I asked Rob for a meeting. I intimidated him into changing his will. I threatened to expose his relationship with your mother. I knew I had to do something to ensure Rob didn't change the will back, so I poisoned him.

"And then Tamara Hayes, always interested in buying the company, started snooping around. I felt she was getting too close. I went to her place to have a conversation with her about her snooping. I guess she thought I was intimidating because she changed her will too. She made me the primary heir. Things progressed to a point that I knew she couldn't be allowed to live, so I poisoned her too. It was easy."

"What you're saying is that Mom and I are accessories after the fact or maybe even accomplices."

"That's right, sweetheart. You have no choice but to stay silent. I have to get out of here before that smart detective figures out that I was here. I have my passport, so I'm headed to Canada."

CHAPTER 44

W hen Detective Conner left an interview, he always liked to sit for a few minutes in his car to think about what he had heard. Something in this case was just not right. He felt that the women were not telling the whole truth or at least hiding something.

He called Flores and told him what he thought. After he heard what Conner had to say, Flores told him to have backup come without lights or sirens.

When they came, Conner sent two patrolmen around to the back of the house, two more to each side of the house, and one with him in the front. "Come out, Davis," Conner yelled through a bullhorn he had in his car. "I know you're in there."

There was nothing but silence. Conner knew they were all still in the house.

"Ladies, I suggest you come out now with your hands where I can see them. Davis, it would be best if you surrendered now."

"Why? So you can put me back in jail? No thanks."

"Surrender for your own good, Davis. No one wants to hurt you, and you'll get a fair trial."

"Yeah, I've heard that one before. You'd manufacture and manipulate evidence to railroad me."

"Davis, you know that's not true. Even if the evidence points to you, you'll still get a fair trial. If the evidence isn't there, you'll be released."

Shots rang out from the back of the house. It was soon a war zone with a cacophony of gunshots. Shortly after the gunfire erupted, it started to abate. Soon, there was no more gunfire.

Conner entered the home through the patio sliding door. The place was a mess; bullet holes dotted the walls, ceilings, and floors. It looked like some of the houses he had seen in Iraq.

Cautiously moving from room to room, Conner found blood trailing off into the bedroom areas. Following the blood, Conner opened the first bedroom door. Inside, he found Veronica bleeding heavily. He called for one of the patrolmen to get in there and help her as much as possible. He told another patrolman to call for ambulances.

Continuing to the next room, Conner found Clara fatally wounded. She had crawled into the room after being shot through and through in her upper chest, where a bullet had nicked her aorta.

Very cautiously, Conner went into the master bedroom. Davis lay near an open window quite dead. He had several wounds any one of which would have been fatal.

CHAPTER 45

Veronica was rushed to the hospital in critical condition due to multiple gunshot wounds; doctors and nurses worked feverishly to save her life. Once stabilized and out of surgery, she was put in the ICU under twenty-four-hour watch. It was doubtful that she would live through the night.

In the aftermath of the deaths of Tom Davis and Clara Barton, Rob sued for his father's will to be declared void because of the deaths and because Davis had coerced Rob's father into changing his will. The judge who had thrown out Rob's first request looked at the evidence and declared the will to be null and void. She reinstated the original will that had been filed with Robert Sr.'s lawyer, which meant that Rob was given the majority of his father's company. His sister and brother each received 15 percent of the stock. Clara Barton was to receive 5 percent, but that went to her daughters. Rob's mother was to receive 10 percent, giving Rob a controlling interest of 55 percent.

Rob didn't immediately start changing the company; he had other priorities. He had to find a new secretary, security chief, and accountant. He also visited Veronica in the hospital.

Madeline was happy that she had received so much of the company because it was more than she would have had if the handwritten will had stood. Her husband wanted to divorce her because he would get half of her inheritance, so he sued her for divorce.

When the divorce papers were served, Madeline made a mad dash to her personal trainer, broke down, and cried. She threw herself into his arms and collapsed. He didn't know what to do, so he just held her for a minute. She finally started to calm down. He asked her what was wrong.

"My husband is suing me for a divorce. That's what's wrong!" she said almost screaming.

"So why's that such a big deal?"

"It's a big deal because he'll get half of everything. I think I'll be able to keep the house because Daddy gave that to me in the will, but I'll have to sell my shares in Daddy's company and give half to Harry."

"How much is it worth?"

"I'm not sure. It could be in the millions."

"You're kidding, right?"

"No. I'm pretty sure it'll be that much. Daddy was very successful. With Rob now running the company, it should do even better."

"I think you'd better get yourself a lawyer, perhaps your father's attorney, to look at the possibilities and help you decide what's best."

"Yeah. You're probably right. I'll call him right away."

While Madeline was making that call, Rory was in the Do Drop Inn drinking as usual and buying rounds for others. And Vivian was also happy about the outcome. She had a continuous flow of money and didn't have to worry about the upkeep of the house or how she was going to replace her wardrobe. She called Jason.

"Jason, this is Viv. How are you doing? I'm very lonely. I wish you were here. Can you quit work a little early and come over?"

"Hello, Viv. I was just thinking about you. It's almost quitting time anyway. I don't see why I can't slip out and come over. What have you got in mind? Do you want to go out for dinner? Maybe take in a movie?"

"No. I want to have a quiet dinner here and a cozy evening in front of the fireplace. I want to have your arms around me. I need to know that you care about me."

"You know I care. I think I'm crazy about you. I can't stop thinking about you. Is that what love is?"

"Jason! Are you saying you love me?"

"Yeah, I guess I am."

"How sweet! Hurry over. I may have a surprise for you."

Jason went to Harold and said, "Harold, I was wondering if I could call it a day. I'm all caught up with my cases."

"Sure, I don't see why not. Gotta hot date?"

"You might say that. See ya tomorrow, bright and early."

CHAPTER 46

Jason hustled out of the office before Harold could ask him who the date was. He got into his car and turned off his cell phone; he didn't want to be disturbed or called back to the office. He was aware that Vivian was in a frisky mood.

He drove to Vivian's house. When he arrived at the gate, it opened without his having to speak into to the speaker. He drove through the gate and watched it close behind him in the rearview mirror. He continued around the circular drive to the front door.

He parked and walked up the steps to the porch. Before he had the opportunity to knock, the door sprung open as if someone had been waiting behind it. Vivian stood just inside the door looking at him appraisingly. She was clothed in a diaphanous sheath that barely covered her lithesome body. Her long blond hair flowed loose to her shoulders. Her makeup applied with care highlighted her sparkling, azure eyes. In a word, she was breathtaking.

Jason stood there staring at her. He thought, *Wow! This is some woman!*

"Aren't you going to come in?" Vivian asked.

Jason stuttered as he mumbled, "Yeah … Yeah … Sure," but he just stood there.

Vivian pulled Jason in by the arm, hugged him, and smothered him with kisses. When she broke the kiss, both were panting breathlessly.

"Wow, Viv! You sure know how to greet a fella and make him feel welcome. Do you do that to all the men who visit you?"

"No, Jason, you're the only one. I never even greeted Robert that way. I think I was saving it for you. Well come in. Are you ready for some fun?"

"I don't know if I can handle any more fun, but yes, I'm ready."

Vivian tugged on his arm and practically dragged him into her bedroom.

CHAPTER 47

Rob went to the hospital to visit Veronica. He didn't know why, but he was concerned about her. She was his half-sister after all. He had met her just a few weeks earlier. He hadn't even known she existed. Rob asked at the nurses' station if there had been any change in her condition. The charge nurse told him no, that she was still in a medically induced coma. Rob told the nurse he wanted to see her anyway.

He walked over to her door and hesitated. He was unsure what to expect. Taking a big breath, he entered the room and was shocked by the array of tubes and wires in and around Ronnie—breathing tubes, feeding tubes, IVs full of fluids, and monitors all working to keep her alive. He was stunned by her beauty and her peaceful appearance. He had been told that people in a coma could hear and understand without seeming to. He started to talk softly to her. Not knowing much about her, he didn't know what to say, so he just said what came to his mind.

"Ronnie, I know I met you only a few weeks ago. I didn't even know you existed. Perhaps had I known, your and your sister's lives would have been different. At any rate, I pledge to take care of the two of you. I'm kinda surprised to find out I have two more sisters. I don't want you to go without. Maybe I can move Samantha closer so we can visit her more often. I'm going to visit her later this afternoon. I hope you don't mind."

Rob didn't feel he was getting through to Ronnie. He decided to try something he had heard about. He gently took one of her hands in his. "Ronnie, can you respond by squeezing my hand? I really hope you get better soon. I'd like to get to know you. Would that be okay?" He waited for a squeeze but didn't feel anything. "Ronnie, are you comfortable?" Still no response. "Is there anything I can do for you?" He thought he felt a slight movement. He asked again, "Can I do anything for you?" He definitely felt a movement though it was light.

"Did you just answer me?" Another movement, stronger that time. Rob grew excited. "What can I do for you, Ronnie? Do you want another pillow?" No response. "Do you want your head raised or lowered?" A slight squeeze. "Which is it? Do you want your head lowered?" No response. "I guess you want your head raised a bit." Squeeze. "Okay, now we're getting somewhere." Rob raised the head of the bed slightly. "Is that okay?" No response. "Do you want it more?" Squeeze. Rob started to raise the head of the bed again. He moved slowly keeping her hand in his. She squeezed when she was more comfortable. "Wow! That's great, Ronnie!"

Rob kept holding her hand and chattering away. At times, he thought he saw eye movement. He kept talking for an hour. He didn't want to tire her out. Also, he wanted to go see his other new sister. Before he left, he asked her, "Would it be all right if I tell Samantha about having a new family?" Squeeze, stronger that time, and she held it for a lot longer. He thought he saw a tear rolling down her cheek. "I'm so sorry. I didn't mean to make you cry." He dried her tears and then left. He went to visit Samantha.

CHAPTER 48

O ver the next several days, Rob visited his new sisters every day. He talked incessantly to Ronnie holding her hand and getting responses though hand squeezing. They were getting stronger and didn't take as long to come.

Finally, one day, when Rob came to visit, the doctors took Ronnie out of her medically induced coma. She was sitting up in bed and alert. She smiled when he went into her room. "Hello, Rob! It's great to see you again."

"Well, this is a pleasant surprise. How are you feeling?"

"I'm doing fine. A little bored, but I think I'll be getting out of the ICU today. I really appreciate your coming to see me even though I couldn't talk to you. Your visits meant the world to me," Ronnie said with tears in her eyes.

"I felt that you needed someone here especially since your mother had been killed. You do remember the raid, don't you?"

"Yeah. I know that's why I'm here. I hadn't known that Mom died though."

She started weeping. Rob rushed over to her reaching for her hand. He wiped her tears away and told her everything would be all right.

"Rob, did you mean what you said while I was in a coma? About my sister and me?"

"About taking care of you? I meant every word. I was waiting to move Sam until after you were released from here so you could help me find a place closer to your home. As far as you're concerned, I have a job for you at Vanderburgh Electronics if you want it."

"Really? Are you kidding me now? What did you have in mind?"

"You're a CPA, aren't you? I need an accountant. My father had kept the books, and I'm no numbers wiz. I need someone I can trust to help me out in that area. Do you think you'd be able to?"

"Sure. I'm a pretty good accountant if I do say so myself. When Mom had inherited the company, she wanted me to keep her books. This will work out perfectly. When will I start? And at what salary?"

"You're very anxious, aren't you? You don't have to start until you're ready. What salary? I was thinking a hundred thousand a year. How's that sound?"

"That's fine, boss. If I get out of ICU today, I can start on auditing the books if you'd bring them in."

A nurse and doctor came in. "Sir, you're going to have to leave now," the nurse said. "We're moving Ms. Vanderburgh to a room now."

"Can you make sure it's a private room for my sister? Maybe a comfortable chair for her to sit in? Don't worry about the cost. I'm covering it."

"Yes sir. All our rooms are private."

"I also want it to be in a quiet area, not near the nurses' station or the elevators. If the room you're planning on taking her to doesn't meet these requirements, she'll just have to stay here until you have a room that does."

Rob and Ronnie talked as they waited for the nurse to return with good news. "Okay, Mr. Vanderburgh, your sister can have a large room at the end of the hall. It's really almost a suite, a very nice room."

The nurse got Ronnie up to the floor and settled into a great room with a widescreen TV and an easy chair. When Rob was sure that Ronnie was settled in and comfortable, he left the hospital to visit Samantha.

CHAPTER 49

T hough she would have to split her inheritance with her husband, Madeline thought she would make the most of it. She would force her husband to move out of their house, which her father had left to her, and have her boy toy move in; then she could have him anytime she wanted. It was a fine plan. She skipped happily to the gym to tell her trainer the good news.

Grinning foolishly, she arrived at the gym and asked for her trainer. When he came around the corner, she knew something was wrong. To her surprise, he stormed out of the back frowning and lit into her. "What are you doing here? You're not scheduled until next week!"

She was taken aback by his vehemence. She thought he would be pleased to see her.

"I wanted to surprise you, and I have a question for you."

"You surprised me. What do you want? I'm busy with another client."

"I knew you might be busy, but this is important. Since my husband and I are getting a divorce, I thought it would be nice if you moved in with me."

"Are you crazy? What you're asking is for me to give up my freedom to work with my other clients."

"You could still work with them. I'd just want you home in the evening."

"That's what I mean. I sometimes service them in the evening."

"What do you mean you service them?"

"Well, you know … Service … Like I do with you."

"I see. That would have to stop of course!"

"I have to get back to my client. Have a nice life, Madeline." He walked away leaving her standing there and staring.

She turned in a huff pouting. She had to figure out what to do. It hit her like a ton of bricks. Of course, she would get another boy toy. That would show him she wasn't one to be trifled with.

Try as she might, Madeline was unable to find a suitable replacement for her trainer. Either they were interested in her only as a sex object or they wanted to be supported by her. What she wanted and needed was to be held, consoled, and comforted.

She went back to her trainer's gym to beg him to come back to her. He agreed with the condition that she wouldn't hold him responsible for a more permanent relationship such as moving in with her. He also demanded that she schedule her appointments with him. She readily agreed to those conditions.

CHAPTER 50

Robert heard that Tamarac Electronics had reverted to Tamara Hayes's mother, father, and brother because of the nullified will, and he learned that they had no background in business or electronics. He could wait and watch them fail or offer them a lowball number for the company.

His first target would be the mother and father since they owned fifty-one percent; he decided to offer them ten bucks a share, around five million dollars. If that didn't work, he would go as high as ten million. He estimated the shares they held were worth somewhere near fifty million, and he hoped they were ignorant about the worth of their stack. Tamara's brother on the other hand was savvy to stock prices though he had no experience in business. Rob hoped he would be able to persuade the parents to sell before the brother got wind of it.

Rob called upon the Hayeses at Tamarac's offices. Walking into the building, Rob saw that the place was pristine. Mauve carpets covered the floors. The elevator doors gleamed; it looked like they were polished every day. A young woman sat at a dark mahogany reception desk; she had long blond hair, brilliant azure eyes, and a peaches-and-cream complexion. She smiled and asked, "May I help you, sir?"

"Yes. My name is Robert Vanderburgh Jr. You may have heard of me."

"Yes sir, I know who you are. How may I help you?"

"I'm here to see Tamara Hayes's parents. Are they here?"

"Yes they are, but they're very busy with the tragedy and all."

"Yes, I can imagine. I come with a business proposal that I think will help them out in a big way. Would you find out if they'll see me?"

"One moment, sir."

She picked up the phone, dialed an extension, and said, "Sir, Robert Vanderburgh is here to see you. Shall I send him in?"

Robert heard a response that sounded angry. The receptionist hung up. She composed herself then said, "I'm sorry, sir, Mr. Hayes told me to tell you that he wasn't interested in you or any proposals you have. He thought you had some nerve to approach him at this time of mourning."

"I can appreciate his mourning. I just lost my father. Would you give him my card and have him call me anytime?"

She took the card, looked at it, and placed it on her desk.

Rob left the building. When he was gone, the receptionist placed the card in the trash.

Sitting in his car, Rob, thought about what to do next. He started the car and slowly headed back to his office.

CHAPTER 51

Jason called Vivian from his office. He had some ideas about how to invest her fortune so that it would grow aggressively. The first order of business was to get her power of attorney and place his name on all her accounts so he could move money around without her permission or knowledge. Jason would also start managing her bills.

"Hi, Viv."

"Oh hi, Jason. How are you?"

"When can I see you? Can you meet me at the bank? There are some things we need to take care of. Then maybe we can go to dinner or something."

"Yeah, sure. What's it about? Why the bank?"

"Just some formalities concerning investments I want to do for you. I need your power of attorney to do this. It would be better for me to be on your accounts too. I want to start managing your bills as well."

Vivian was concerned about giving Jason her power of attorney and putting him on her accounts. She thought she could trust him, but she had met him so recently and didn't really know him well. He did work for the family's attorney, so he had to be trustworthy, *Right?*

She met the bank manager in the lobby. "Hello, Mrs. Vanderburgh. It's good to see you again. I understand you want Jason to be added to your accounts and you're giving him power of attorney. You do know you can give him limited power of attorney, so that won't have the ability to go willy-nilly. I can help you with that if you wish," the banker said.

"Jason is an attorney, so I imagine he's already drafted one."

"More than likely. Make sure you read it carefully. Let me know if you have any questions."

They went into the manager's office, where Jason was waiting.

"Hi! Viv. You look great!" Jason said. He stood to greet her, kissed her cheeks, and held a chair out for her. He sat as did the bank manager.

"Shall we get started?" Jason asked. "The first order of business is to get your late husband's name off your accounts and add mine."

Looking at the banker, he asked, "Do you have the signature cards ready?" To Vivian, he said, "This is just a formality. It'll allow me to move funds around without pestering you."

Vivian glanced at the banker, who almost imperceptivity nodded. She then looked at the signature cards. Her name was typed below the signature line, and Jason's name was typed below the next line. She signed it and handed it to Jason, who signed it with a flourish.

Jason handed Vivian the power of attorney and said, "This will give me the ability to buy and sell your stocks as I see fit to invest your money more aggressively."

"Okay, Jason. I want to read it if you don't mind."

"No, I don't mind. In fact, I insist."

Vivian read the power of attorney and asked some questions for clarification. She then signed it with the admonition that she wanted monthly reports on how she was doing financially.

They left the bank, drove to Vivian's house, and relaxed while dinner was prepared by the cook. Jason was excited about the prospect of growing Viv's wealth. He told her he was going to invest a quarter of her money in money markets and another quarter would be in stocks and bonds with the rest staying where it was for liquidity.

They enjoyed a scrumptious dinner of shrimp alfredo and coffee. For dessert, they had banana cream pie. After dinner, they went into the den, watched a little TV, then retired for the night.

CHAPTER 52

Veronica Vanderburgh visited her sister every day hoping to see Rob there. She knew it was wrong, but she was infatuated with him.

One day, she found him there reading to her sister. She said, "Hi, Rob. It's nice to see you."

His heart started beating rapidly at the sound of her voice. "Hey, Ronnie. I was hoping I'd see you today. I was just reading to our sister," Rob said.

Ronnie's heart sank at the reminder of their relationship. "Yes, I see. What are you reading?"

"One of my all-time favorites, *Of Mice and Men*, by John Steinbeck. I'm not sure she understands."

"It's all right. She probably enjoys the sound of your voice. I know I do."

"Thank you. I know it's inappropriate, but I wish we weren't related, Ronnie."

"Really? Me too."

"You're kidding, aren't you?"

"No. I wish we could find out that we weren't brother and sister."

"There is a way. We could get our DNA tested."

"Do you want to?"

"Sure. Why not? What would it harm?"

"I don't think it would harm anything. We'd find out the truth of our relationship."

"How disappointed will you be if we turn out to be brother and sister?" Rob asked.

"A little, I suppose."

"Are you sure you want to do this?"

"Yes. Do you have any idea where we could go?"

They asked the head nurse if he knew of any place. The nurse told them they could use 23 and me, but that would take weeks to get the results back. He suggested that maybe the nursing home doctor would order the test for the three of them.

They asked Dr. Smythe, and she agreed. The doctor ordered the DNA testing to be done stat. The nurse swabbed the sisters' and Rob's mouths and immediately sent the samples off to the lab. They waited for the results nervously and eagerly. Rob continued reading to Samantha as Ronnie paced the room and then the hallway. Ronnie came back with two cups of coffee. Hers had light cream and sugar. His was hot, black, and strong, and when he joked about its being just like his women, Ronnie glared at him.

About an hour later, the nurse stuck his head in the room to see if they needed anything.

"Can I get you folks anything? Coffee? Tea?" He grinned at Ronnie. "Or me?"

"The results of the test would be nice," Ronnie said nervously.

"Yes ma'am. The test takes about three hours to complete once the lab has the samples. They picked up the samples nearly half an hour ago."

"I wish they'd hurry up."

"Ronnie, if it turns out that we're not brothers and sisters, I'll continue to support and care for Samantha. I don't want you to worry about that," Rob said.

Ronnie replied, "That's very generous of you. Which way do you want the results to go?"

"Are you serious? I didn't think there was any doubt about

how I feel. I like the idea of having two more sisters, but I think things would be a lot less complicated if we weren't related."

Ronnie's heart fluttered. She lowered her eyes demurely and blushed. "Me too."

They silently contemplated about what would change if the results showed that they were not related.

An hour later, the nurse came back into the room followed by the doctor. The doctor had an envelope in her hand. She looked very serious. "These are the result of the DNA testing. Are you absolutely certain you want to know what this report says?"

They exclaimed simultaneously, "Yes!"

"Don't keep us in suspense any longer," exclaimed Rob.

"All right," the doctor said as she opened the envelope. "Hmm. This is interesting. It says that Rob and Samantha are most likely related but that Ronnie isn't related to Rob."

Veronica was so shocked to hear that she was not Samantha's sister that she almost passed out. She sat down quickly breathing hard. "What? I don't understand. What does that mean?"

Dr. Smythe took Ronnie's hand and gently said, "It appears that you and Samantha had different fathers. Rob's father and your mother had a union that produced Sam. Since the results show that you and Sam are siblings and Rob and Sam are siblings but you aren't Rob's sibling, it would follow that you had a different father."

Veronica and Robert were ecstatic. They had spent the last several weeks together visiting Samantha at the nursing home. They had fallen in love with each other. Because they were not related after all, they could consummate that love without guilt.

They left the nursing home walking slowly and close to each other. They got to Ronnie's car and turned to each other. They took each other's hands. Ronnie peered into Rob's beautiful azure eyes and asked, "What now?"

Rob pulling her closer and wrapped her in his arms. "I just

want to be with you. I don't care what anybody says. We were meant to be together."

"I agree with you. Since we're not related, there's no reason for us not to be together. Do you want to go home or have dinner?"

"We should probably eat dinner. I have the feeling this will be a long, memorable, enjoyable night."

They decided to go to Rob's home and drop off Ronnie's car. Then they went to a favorite Japanese restaurant. There they sat so close their legs touched. They held hands and gazed into each other's eyes.

Back at Rob's house, they sat in the car in the driveway like a couple of teenagers. Finally, Rob suggested they go inside.

The next morning, Rob went to work while Ronnie went to the nursing home to visit her half-sister. On the way, she thought about the previous night and smiled.

Printed in the United States
By Bookmasters